"You should lock your door when you're in the tub," Cullen said.

"Aargh!" Krystal sloshed water over the sides of the tub as she fought for control of her mind and body. Cullen! Had she conjured him up by wanting him so much?

"Shall I wash you?" he asked.

Startled, she sank back into the masses of bubbles. "Get out of here!" she insisted, sneaking a peek at him. That wonderful body . . . how dare he seduce her with his looks? She'd have him arrested for being a pervert—right after she'd kissed him about six or seven thousand times. "Leave."

"Calm down," Cullen said soothingly. "It's me." He gazed at her creamy pink body and thought he'd have his first heart attack. She was incredibly beautiful, strong and shapely. The sight of her made him crazy, just as her absence had. He'd scrawled her initials on memos and faxes, even called his partner Krystal by mistake. She just had to talk to him—she was wrecking his life, and he needed her.

"Cullen, you trespasser, voyeur, burglar—"

"Quiet down, they can hear you on the docks. You left the door unlocked."

"Get out of here, you—"

"I'll get you out of there first. In the mood you're in, you could slip and fall," he said.

"Hand me a towel, then wait in the other room." How could she get out while he was there, looking too darn sexy? She splashed water at him. "Get out, Cullen."

"We have to talk, Krystal," he said, then reached down and lifted her straight out of the tub. . . .

WHAT ARE *LOVESWEPT* ROMANCES?

They are stories of true romance and touching emotion. We believe those two very important ingredients are constants in our highly sensual and very believable stories in the *LOVESWEPT* line. Our goal is to give you, the reader, stories of consistently high quality that may sometimes make you laugh, sometimes make you cry, but are always fresh and creative and contain many delightful surprises within their pages.

Most romance fans read an enormous number of books. Those they truly love, they keep. Others may be traded with friends and soon forgotten. We hope that each *LOVESWEPT* romance will be a treasure—a "keeper." We will always try to publish

LOVE STORIES YOU'LL NEVER FORGET
BY AUTHORS YOU'LL ALWAYS REMEMBER

The Editors

Helen Mittermeyer
Krystal

BANTAM BOOKS
NEW YORK · TORONTO · LONDON · SYDNEY · AUCKLAND

KRYSTAL

A Bantam Book / January 1992

*If you would be interested in receiving protective vinyl
covers for your Loveswept books, please write to this address
for information:*

> Loveswept
> Bantam Books
> P.O. Box 985
> Hicksville, NY 11802

ISBN 0-553-44214-7

Published simultaneously in the United States and Canada

---

*Bantam Books are published by Bantam Books, a division
of Bantam Doubleday Dell Publishing Group, Inc. Its trade-
mark, consisting of the words "Bantam Books" and the
portrayal of a rooster, is Registered in U.S. Patent and Trade-
mark Office and in other countries. Marca Registrada.
Bantam Books, 666 Fifth Avenue, New York, New York 10103.*

PRINTED IN THE UNITED STATES OF AMERICA

OPM   0 9 8 7 6 5 4 3 2 1

To my four children, who have tested the theory of shock proof on me. I think I'm almost there.

One

He saw the curl first and blinked.

Red-gold and silken, it was incongruous with the janitorial, snoodlike head gear that held her hair to the back of her head. He couldn't see the face. Yet.

Cullen Hughson Dempsey was exhausted, and scarcely knew night from day. Seeing things wouldn't have been strange. How could he be sure of a red-gold curl? He blinked again. It was still there, and coming closer.

He rolled his shoulders and rubbed his neck to loosen the stiffness. Yawning, he stared again at the curl that swung back and forth as the person, head down, slowly swept a soapy-wet mop across the floor. It had to be a woman, he thought. No cruel fate would let a male have such magical strands. And a fairly young woman, judging by the smooth-skin of her cheek. Why would a young woman be washing floors at night? Times were tough, but . . .

The only time her hypnotic motion changed was when she rinsed the mop, wringing it out and dipping it into the soapy water, then beginning her ritual again. Back and forth. Swish, slap, mop, steadily toward him.

Cullen inhaled deeply, smothering another yawn. Absently he wondered why she didn't use a scrubbing machine. It would be easier, but was perhaps too expensive?

The long journey from Kamchatka Peninsula, USSR, to San Jose, California, then on to his new base of operations in Seattle, Washington, had made him almost unbearably travel-weary. He'd only been settled in his new offices a week before he'd made the three-week junket to the Soviet Union, then gone on to finish closing up his offices in San Jose. Dempsey Fisheries, Inc. was now located in an upside-down, icicle-shaped building overlooking Pike's Market and the island-studded Puget Sound. He liked the view, the city, the people . . . and he liked reddish-gold curls.

Cullen didn't usually work after midnight at any time. His philosophy was to work hard, but sensibly, since playing hard was almost as important to him. Such a philosophy had granted him a measure of financial success, and he was now able to enter into lucrative international contracts—such as with the Russians, who would market his fish as he marketed theirs. Things were on an upward curve, and that included the decision to relocate to Seattle. But the move had created some problems, a few lost files, some irate letters that needed handling, a couple of employees with ruffled feathers that needed to be smoothed . . . So, he'd worked late this night.

The noise out in the corridor had drawn him from his office, though, and that's when he'd spotted the shiny twist of hair. Now he was reluctant to leave the red-gold curl until he saw the face behind it. He stifled another yawn and propped his shoulder against the door jamb.

Slap! Swish! Plop! The slow rhythmic strokes brought her ever closer. He didn't take his eyes off the curl. Hair that beautiful didn't usually come with the floor scrubbers he'd seen. Most of them had been men, and the few women had been well into middle age.

When she raised one arm to wipe her perspiring face on her sleeve, she saw him. Startled, she reared back, grasping the mop in front of her with both hands. Surprise as well as a lacing of trepidation and wariness flashed across her features.

"Hi," Cullen said quickly. "I didn't mean to frighten you. I'm Cullen Dempsey, and I've just moved into the building. Generally, I don't work this late. I had to straighten out some files."

Why was he explaining to her, he asked himself, this lady with the beautiful skin, and the smudges on her forehead and nose? Maybe because he'd seen her fear, and he wondered about that.

"Oh." Heart thudding out of rhythm, Krystal Wynter stared at the man. Had she ever met him? No. He wasn't the least bit familiar. None the less, she scrutinized him again. It paid to make sure. One of the advantages of working nights was the solitude. She craved it. That was why she'd started the office-cleaning business in the first place. As a rule she met fewer people at night, and those she met were complete strangers. That suited her just fine. No. This man was a new one. And a hunk. That's how some of her staff would've described him. Those broad shoulders, long legs, and strong thighs belonged on a linebacker, not a business-man. And his hands looked rough, the skin chapped and maybe even callused. His fine blue business suits didn't go with those rough hands. Who was he?

"Go right ahead with your work, sir," she said. She flapped her hand at his office, hoping he'd take the hint and disappear. "I'll be done here in short order and I shouldn't disturb you."

Dammit, she thought. He wasn't moving. He was big and determined-looking, with deep blue eyes and hair black as midnight, short on top and touching his collar at the back. As well groomed and natty as he was, had she seen him on the street, she would have bet he was a stevedore or lumberman. Muscles bunched right through his suit. He was a damned Paul Bunyan. Maybe, she thought giddily, he'd parked his blue ox Babe in the underground garage. Gad! She was getting light-headed from doing two workers' jobs. Who would have guessed that the flu would hit at Christmastime? And the snow! It always rained in Seattle, but two feet of snow? Never. Yet they had it. Her van's almost-bald tires were having a heyday skidding whenever she drove. That eve-ning, rather than risk it, she'd carted her equip-ment on the bus in a large two-wheeled basket she could pull behind her.

"I'm in no hurry," Cullen said. He'd seen her quickly masked disappointment when he hadn't immediately returned to his office. He might have retreated if she hadn't been so patently eager to get rid of him. And if she weren't so intriguing. She was a looker. Her face was heart-shaped, and her eyes, which were a brilliant emerald green and slanted upward at the corners, were almost too big for it. She could have modeled with that face and coloring. And he would bet her body was good too. Though she wore shapeless coveralls and was leaning on her mop handle, he could tell her body was trim and in good shape. He could believe she was a model. An actress. A business manager. Even an entrepreneur—if she had the smarts—but instead she cleaned offices. Strange choice for an attractive young woman, he mused. And he had a real hankering to see her without the baggy coveralls. "And your name?" he asked.

"Mine?" Krystal didn't divulge her name, address, or social security number to anyone other than possible clients if she could help it. Anonymity worked the best.

"Yours," he said implacably.

"I'm KT Wynter of KT Office Cleaning. I'm filling in for one of my workers who has the flu. Strange weather for Seattle, isn't it? None of us expected snow this Christmas. Usually we get rain, not two feet of snow." She was babbling, stumbling over words as though they were boulders strewn in her path. That had happened to her ever since leaving San Francisco two years ago. She tried to avoid people whenever possible, and when she couldn't, she was bumbling and unsure. Nothing made her more uncomfortable than questions.

Cullen moved toward her, noticing her infinitesimal step back. "Have you a long stretch to go?" He saw how warily she watched him, how she seemed to factor what he said and weigh her answer.

"Ah, yes," she said. "I'll be working for hours yet."

"So will I. Let me know when you're done, and I'll walk you down to the garage." She looked so startled at his statement, he wondered what kinds of men she knew? Something, someone, had made her unusually skittish.

"No need," she said. "I still have to do the fifth floor and—"

"Fine," he interrupted, determined not to let her get away. "I'll give you my number and you can call me when you're finished. I have enough to keep me busy." He didn't try to rationalize why he was pressuring the cleaning woman. Returning to his office, he copied down the phone number that he hadn't yet memorized or had cards for, and took the piece of paper out to the unsettled and unsettling janitor. Pressing the paper into her hand, he smiled. Before she could formulate a protest, he reentered the office, closed the door, and leaned against it, chuckling.

Krystal stared at the scrap of paper, then at the door, then back to the paper. What had happened? She'd been minding her own business, scrubbing along, wondering if she'd collect the money due from a few clients the next day, then . . . bam! That steamroller had appeared in front of her, rolled right over the top of her, and disappeared as quickly as he'd come. She crushed the piece of paper and jammed it into the pocket of her cover-all. She'd forget about him. Once she was done on five, her last floor, she'd leave, on her own, by herself.

Trying to put Cullen Dempsey out of her mind, however, was easier said than done. While she scrubbed the last corridor, he danced around her brain like a mosquito. No matter how hard she swatted at him, he continued pestering her, sting-ing her.

Finally finished, thirsty, and hungry, she washed and rinsed her equipment and put it away. She knew she'd be the last of her staff in the building, because she'd taken on the extra floor. Yawning, she went to the ladies room on the fifth floor, used the facility, and washed as much of the surface dirt off her as she could. She'd shower at home.

After loading her wheeled carryall, she took the elevator down to the basement. That was where her locker was, and she was pretty sure Tall, Dark, and Persistent would forget about what he'd said, forget about her. In case he hadn't, she could avoid him there, since most of it was for the building's maintenance workers only. From the basement it was only a short walk to the parking garage, then up the ramp to the bus stop half a block away.

In the locker room she stripped off her soiled coveralls, rolling them up and putting them in a plastic bag, along with the hair net she'd worn. Before sleeping that night, she'd wash her cover-alls, so they'd be ready to wear the following evening.

Not able to control her yawns, she took her

slacks and blouse from the locker, shook out the wrinkles, and donned them. Though they were slightly wilted, they'd do for the bus ride home through the after-midnight sleepiness of the city.

After putting on her coat, boots, hat, and gloves, she grabbed her purse and the bag on wheels. Shaking her head to clear it, she opened the door to the cavernous hall that led to the parking garage. She cautiously checked that she was alone—a habit she'd gotten into since having begun to work nights—then strode swiftly along the hall. Her rubber-soled boots made a thunking sound on the concrete floor. The yellowish lights gave the hall an eerie glow, and more than once she glanced over her shoulder.

She sighed when she reached the door at the end of the hall, longing to be home and in the shower. She opened the door, revealing the stairs that led down to the parking garage, and a damp coldness assailed her. She shivered. It always made her nervous to cross the dark garage, but it was the quickest exit to the street.

She was on the third step down when she heard the noise. Pausing, she took a deep breath and shifted her bundles so she could remove an atomizer from her bag. It was filled with a solution of ammonia and water. She removed the cap and dropped her purse and gloves into the cart, leaving her right hand free. Then, moving slowly, she shifted her cart down the last steps to the door at the bottom.

She yanked down on the security handle of the steel door and opened it, nudging her cart through first and looking right and left before following it quickly.

"Hello. Planning to Mace someone?"

"Aaagh!" Krystal jumped back, right against the door. "You scared me," she said accusingly to Cullen Dempsey. "I don't like people sneaking up on me."

"I didn't," he said pleasantly. "Have you had a bad experience with a stranger?"

"Hasn't everyone?"

"I haven't."

"Lucky you. How did you know I was done?" It was a mere thirty feet to the exit from the garage, she thought. And she'd been on the track team in high school.

"I took a chance you'd be down here when you weren't on five." He smiled when he saw her frown. "You mentioned that five was your last floor."

"Did I?" Shifting her cart around to one side so that she could pick it up when she ran, she eased around him.

"Can I give you a lift somewhere?" he asked. "You look loaded down."

"No thanks."

Jumping forward, she shot around him and raced for the short set of steps up to the street. She was out of breath from panic and the weight of the cart when she reached them, but she didn't pause. It was on the last step that she either got careless or miscalculated. Her boot caught on the edge and slid on the slickness left by the snow. When she tried to save herself, her other foot slipped on the icy pavement. Flailing, she let go of the cart. It fell one way and she went the other, landing facedown in a pile of dirty snow that had been cleared from the walk, still clutching her atomizer.

Strong arms lifted her from behind. "First, Miss KT Wynter," Cullen said, "I am not a rapist, nor a thief. I don't prey on women, and I apologize if I scared you." He stood her on her feet, fetched her cart and the small pieces of equipment that had scattered out of it, then faced her.

She tried to wipe her face clean and spit snow from her mouth at the same time. "All right," she said, nodding slowly. "I'm cautious. It's a habit."

"And a good one, if it doesn't drive you to paranoia."

"If that's how you see it," she said stiffly, donning her gloves before reaching for her things. Her hands were stiff, wet, and very cold.

"Don't be so damned touchy. I'm not intimating anything, or making a move on you."

Feeling teary and foolish, with one elbow stinging from having hit the cement support, she glared up at him, fighting for control. "Thanks for getting my things."

"Look, you're upset, and I'm feeling a little guilty about that. You wouldn't have run or slipped if you hadn't been trying to get away from me. Let me drive you home. I'll see you to your door and go. I don't like leaving you like this." He smiled and swiped more snow off her coat. "I suppose I could be putting myself at risk. If you decided to yell for a cop, I could be in trouble."

"I—I won't do that. But I can get home by myself. The bus stop is right there." She pointed to the corner. "And it takes me right to my street."

"Let me make amends by driving you. No strings,"

he said quickly. She was more than cautious, he mused, again wondering what might have happened to her. When she nodded shortly, he took her cart and her arm. "You keep the Mace and purse. Let's go."

"Mace is illegal. This is ammonia and water."

Krystal followed him back down the steps, her legs feeling rubbery. She smothered the inner voice that told her he could still be a rapist. What did she know about him? She was too tired to answer her own question.

She consoled herself by thinking that the drive to her house wouldn't take long. She had the third floor of a house not too far from the downtown area. It wasn't a new house, by any means. In fact, it was pretty ramshackle, but her landlady was amiable and she had the whole floor to herself, which consisted of one good-sized room and a bathroom. The view from her narrow attic windows was not spectacular—downtown and office buildings—but if she leaned a certain way out her bathroom window, she could see a portion of Mt. Rainier. She loved that. There was a permanence there, a beauty that was hers alone.

Soon she'd be moving, though, and the mere thought of that filled her with elation. She'd be poorer than she was now, but the building was in good shape. The downstairs, which had once been a store, she'd convert into an office and storeroom. Upstairs was an apartment, dirty, dusty, and musty now, but she'd make it better. She felt downright rich.

Cullen unlocked and opened the passenger door to a dark green Jaguar. As she settled in the seat—atomizer still in hand, just in case—he stowed her cart in the trunk. She was so tired and so grateful to be sitting, she was barely aware of him getting into the car and starting the engine.

Cullen glanced at her as he steered the car up the ramp to the street. Her eyes were almost closed. He'd suffered exhaustion enough times to recognize it in her. "You'll have to give me directions," he said softly.

Blinking, she sat up straighter and nodded. "Turn left at the corner, then go down four blocks and turn right." She couldn't nod off, she told herself, not when she was riding with a stranger.

The ride to her home took a matter of minutes. During that weird time between midnight and dawn, few cars were on the streets. Most places were closed. Pedestrians were a rarity. In a few hours the avenues would be clogged with people and vehicles. For now, though, the street was a frosty, foggy pocket of quiet that had a peculiar lonesomeness about it.

When they stopped for a light a half block from her place, Krystal unbuckled her seat belt. "Don't bother turning the corner. I can get out here." She had her hand on the door when he touched her arm.

"It's no problem." He pulled away from the light and turned left, then stopped when she told him to, in front of a large three-story house. It had forty-foot peaks and two tall brick chimneys. Two small balconies sagged drunkenly on the second floor, and along one side was a rusted fire escape.

The paint had blistered and peeled, and a gutter swung loose, creaking rhythmically.

"You go up and unlock the door," Cullen said. "I'll bring your things. Go ahead," he urged her when she hesitated.

Krystal glanced over her shoulder as she unlocked the big glass front door, being careful not to make noise. Along with her widowed landlady, who lived to the left of the entrance, there was an older couple in the right-hand apartment. The two smaller apartments on the second floor were occupied by an engineer and a teacher. Since they worked days, they usually didn't rise until seven or so. Krystal tried to be courteous and quiet in deference to her unknown neighbors.

She put a finger to her lips when Cullen joined her at the door. "I have sleeping neighbors," she whispered. "Thank you." She took the cart, set it beside her, and held out her hand. "You've been very kind."

He shook her hand, smiling wryly. "You're welcome." He seemed about to say more, but instead turned away and walked back down the steps to his car.

Krystal watched him go, not moving until the car pulled away from the curb. Exhaling, she grabbed her dirty coveralls from the cart and started down the stairs to the dark basement, slowly, quietly, trying to avoid the squeaky areas.

She put her laundry in the washing machine, then waited a few minutes to make sure the machine wouldn't try to bossa nova over the concrete floor. She then hurried up to her apartment to do the rest of her chores. She cleaned her equipment, and replaced it in the cart, showered and shampooed, then had a quick tuna sandwich and a glass of milk before hustling back to the basement to retrieve her wash. She hung her coveralls on a hanger in the bathroom. They would be fresh for the next night.

The last thing she did before going to bed was see to her accounts. It looked like she'd just squeak by on the payroll, if the accounting firm paid on time, which it generally did. Though business had picked up and she'd taken on two new customers in the last month, there were still some scary moments financially.

Throughout all of her tasks, the face of the stranger kept popping up in front of her. He was with her when she showered, straightened up, had her sandwich and milk. And he was there when she fell into bed, her eyes closing on his smile.

Cullen Dempsey could be dangerous to her peace of mind, she thought sleepily, because he wasn't predictable. His rugged good looks could hide a Satan. If they did, he was a consummate actor.

She'd never met anyone like him in San Francisco, or during her travels with her father. And at her home, back east, she'd been too absorbed in trying to get an education and help on the farm to have more than passing flirtations.

School seemed a million light years away. Her father seemed like a creature from her imagination. Shuddering, she squeezed her eyes shut and tried to do the same with the memories. Pain was a big part of her past, and she'd gotten used to putting it on the back porch of her mind. The present was all she could handle. And she wanted to sleep through that. She mumbled her prayers with the covers pulled over her head. She wouldn't think of yesterday. Or of the Paul Bunyan of the evening. She wouldn't let it be important in her life. Fatigue blanketed her mind and she was asleep in minutes.

Two

It was funny how she stayed in his mind, Cullen mused a few days later. He had women friends, many of them, in fact, and some he'd had a long time. He'd never made a commitment to a woman, though. He preferred the kind of female who could identify with that. But the cleaning lady with the red-gold curls kept coming back to him, as though entering and leaving his brain through a revolving door.

He hadn't seen her since he'd driven her home, but he'd made inquiries. KT Wynter Cleaning Service was considered a reliable company, but not much was known about the owner. He kept asking, though.

"Della," he said to his new secretary that morning, "tell me about the outfit that cleans the building."

Della Maken stared at him over her half glasses. "Well, I've worked in this building for several years,

16

and I've never met any of them. I suppose that's good. They're supposed to do most of their work at night and not be underfoot during business hours, as I understand it. I think our offices look clean when I come in, so I've no cause to complain." She looked at him inquiringly.

"Thanks." He smiled wryly. He couldn't tell her he was really asking about a cleaning woman with red-gold hair.

Gadsden Worth, Cullen's partner, heard the exchange as he entered Cullen's office. Gadsden still handled the office in Sausalito, but he'd flown up to Seattle that day to help with the transitional problems. "Something not right?" he asked.

Cullen shook his head. "Just wondered if Della knew any of the people at KT Wynter."

"What's so riveting about the janitorial staff?" Gadsden asked. He was an older man, who'd started Dempsey Fisheries many years ago with Cullen's father. Cullen was like a son to him, and he was proud of the young man, who'd taken over the major running of the business several years ago and had expanded and improved it.

"Just wondering," Cullen said. The phone rang, and the incident faded away in the press of business.

At noon, Cullen decided to walk to Pike's Market, grab some fruit, and stroll around while ruminating over his recurring battle with the cleaning woman who'd invaded his brain. The unaccustomed snow made the walking tricky, and he skidded more than once, but he was so delighted with the fresh air, he ignored his occasional slip and slide. At the market, he found a stand and purchased an apple and a banana. Finishing those, he bought a steaming cup of very dark coffee, sniffing appreciatively the rich brew laced with Louisiana chicory.

Wandering back outdoors, he inhaled in satisfaction the chill wind that crossed Elliot Bay. Then he strolled along the wide wharf that was used by the ferries to shuttle workers and sightseers to the islands in Puget Sound. A few sections of the huge wharf had been roped off. Cullen assumed it was because of ice, but he headed in that direction anyway. The air was quite cold but fresh, and it rejuvenated him. There were several other stalwart souls out there, including some mothers with children.

His attention was caught by one particularly active youngster, wrapped to the nose in winter garb. It crossed his mind that the child would bear close watching on the slippery dock.

Then he saw her. She'd been in his mind so much, he thought for a moment he'd imagined her. She was real, though. His gaze riveted on her, he walked toward her. She didn't notice him, for her attention was on the small boy he'd been watching. Then she jolted forward as though yanked by a string. Her mouth opened and closed, but he couldn't hear her.

He could see the sudden alarm on her face, though, and hurried toward her, his gaze darting left and right as he tried to fix on the cause of her fear. She screamed suddenly and threw herself forward. The boy! Realization had him sprinting over the icy dock.

The little boy had toddled away from his mother,

chasing snowflakes and smacking at them with a gloved hand, chuckling at his own efforts. He was on the edge of the dock when his mother turned to him, too far away to grab him as his feet began to slip.

KT reached him in time, though, snagging him. But her mad dash across the ice had unbalanced her. As the child slid toward the edge, she lost her footing.

"No! KT!" Cullen yelled, diving forward. Feeling as though he were moving in slow motion, Cullen knew he wouldn't be in time. She'd unbalanced herself just enough to lose purchase on the slick surface. Her feet kicked out for solid ground, her free hand scrambled for it. Both crying out in terror, woman and child went over the side.

Screams rent the air as Cullen, too, slid over the front of the dock, hands clawing for KT and some sort of anchor. His hand found the shoulder of her jacket and closed, even as his legs screwed around a stanchion and latched tight. They swung in the air precariously. Seconds fled, seeming like hours. He choked in air, tightening his grip, gritting his teeth.

"Hold on to the boy," he managed to say. His arm was being yanked from his shoulder by the combined weight of the child and the woman. His other hand dug and dug again, nails slipping, gouging out ice chips under them. His gloves were long gone.

"I . . . I will," Krystal stammered. She looked up at him, fearful, but holding herself as still as possible. Where had Cullen come from? she wondered. The boy wriggled and started to cry. She tried to shift him so that his snow gear didn't choke him. "Shh, dearest," she murmured, "it's all right. We're going right back to mommy. Be brave." She tried to smile, but all her concentration was on holding the boy without choking him.

Faces appeared above her, one that of a crying woman. She must be the mother, Krystal thought, as a couple of people grabbed hold of the woman, keeping her back from the edge.

People were yelling. Some were screaming.

"How did it happen?"

"He must've gotten under the barrier and slipped."

"Get help."

Shouted questions were interspersed with directions. Men took hold of Cullen, trying to pull him back.

"No!" Cullen yelled. "Anchor me. If you pull too strongly, I could lose my grip on her. Go over the top of me. Somebody get down there with a rope. The boy can't last a minute in the bay." The strain of shouting back to those on the dock made a pulse throb in his forehead. He looked down at KT, swallowing with an effort. "Hang on, KT. We're going to get out of this."

His quiet voice penetrated and she nodded, her throat tight. She tried not to dwell on the fact that she was beginning to lose feeling in the freezing fingers gripping the boy. Were they slipping? God help them. She couldn't lose the child.

Minutes crawled by. The din of shouting increased, the panoply of sound reverberating through the wooden, ice-coated dock. Krystal could make no sense of the words. All her concentration was on the boy as they swung slowly, suspended from Cullen Dempsey's arm.

Then she heard authoritative voices demanding that people move back. Police whistles, and the unmistakable vibration of a vehicle on the wharf. There was a rustling sound, then someone was next to her.

"Easy, lady," the young man said. "Don't move. I'll do it all. I'm from Rescue." She nodded. "Am I still holding him? I'm afraid to look and I can't feel anything." She gulped. "He isn't crying anymore."

"He's all right. His eyes are open and he's watching me. I think he's tired." The man smiled. "You're doing just fine. We'll get the boy first, then you." He spoke soothingly, as though he dangled from a modified boatswain's chair and made conversation over an icy bay every day. He adjusted his position so he was directly in front of the boy, and then, in one quick move, reached out and grasped the child, hooking him under the arms and across the chest. It took him long minutes, though, to pry Krystal's fingers loose, because they'd cramped on the child.

"There," he finally said. "I'll be back, lady."

She wanted to nod that she understood as the man disappeared, but she was afraid to move, even to look up. How had Cullen managed to hold her and the child so long? She'd lost all feeling in her limbs, and her body was shuddering with reaction and cold.

When she felt a jerk on her clothing, she stiffened.

"Easy, KT," Cullen said. "It's all right. They're coming for you."

She could hear the tension in his voice and had to wonder how he was feeling. His arm must have been all but pulled from its socket.

Then hands grasped her and she was being lifted, right past Cullen Dempsey, who smiled at her lopsidedly. She saw that more than half his body was extended off the pier, and three men were holding him in place. "How did he do it?" she asked an attendant who was holding her tightly in front of himself.

He chuckled. "Beats me, lady. He must be Superman. He'll probably need therapy for that shoulder, though. Damn, if he isn't a hero. So are you."

"No!" Krystal shook her head as the man set her down on her feet. Her early life had taught her to be self-effacing; her later years had taught her to hide.

"Easy, easy, now," the man said. "No need to carry on. Why, you're trembling. Not to worry. You're a little shocky, but it'll pass. Let me get you into the ambulance—"

"No. I don't—"

"We have to take you, ma'am. That's the law. Never know what could happen if we left you alone." The man spoke kindly, but his face was determined.

"But, really, I'm fine. I'll sign a waiver—"

"KT." She looked up to see Cullen standing beside her, holding his arm. "It'll be less of a hassle just to go along, then get released. They'll get us back to work."

"I'm not working at the moment," she said, "but I do have errands to run." She knew her voice was rising, and she made an effort to modulate her tones. Before she could say more, she was whisked onto a gurney.

Cullen shook his head when the paramedics tried to put him on a gurney too. Still cradling his right arm, he walked alongside KT as they wheeled her to the ambulance. "It's all right, KT," he said gently. "We'll be on our way in no time."

Biting her lip, Krystal nodded. She didn't want notoriety. It would be too much like San Francisco when her father had been arrested. He'd died before he'd come to trial, but people remembered. She'd discovered that the first time someone spat in her face.

Cheers rang out as they continued down the wharf. Cullen noted how KT started and tried to hide her face, but then she smiled fleetingly as people reached out to touch her arm.

A burly fireman who walked close to Cullen, eyeing him speculatively, and ready to support him if need be, smiled down at KT. "You did a fine job, ma'am. We might've lost that boy without your quick thinking." He grinned at Cullen. "I don't think I'd like to get in one of your holds, Mr. Dempsey. You've got a mighty grip."

"Right now, I couldn't hold a fork," Cullen said, and smiled when the man laughed.

People surged forward, calling out as KT was lifted into the back of the ambulance.

The same fireman touched her arm. "Ma'am, one of the women is the boy's mother. I think she wants to thank you."

A young woman pushed past the fireman, crying, thanking KT, saying she'd see her at the hospital. Then Krystal was looking at the fireman again.

"Anyone else would've done the same," KT said, then quickly turned her face away as a camera flashed.

When the double doors were shut, safely enclosing Cullen, KT, and the paramedic, Cullen saw her mouth quiver, saw the relief in her eyes. Why was KT Wynter afraid? he wondered. He frowned, then winced as the attendant worked on his hand.

"Sorry, sir. I think you have a couple of sprained fingers, but we'll know more at the hospital. This bandaging should make them feel better."

"Thanks." He smiled briefly, then returned his attention to KT. Why was she so frightened? She certainly hadn't been scared when she'd risked her life for the boy. It wasn't his business, but he damn well wanted to know.

When the paramedic asked for her name, address, and business, Krystal gave him the information reluctantly. "Really," she added, "there's no reason to take me to the hospital. You did say the boy was all right."

"Screaming like a banshee for his mother," the attendant said, smiling. "But I think his mother was even more upset than he was. They're in the vehicle ahead of us."

Krystal could see the attendant was going to ignore her request to be let out of the ambulance, so she closed her eyes, biting back a wince when her curled fingers began to throb. Life was coming back to the nerves with a vengeance. She gritted her teeth against the pain.

But even that didn't dim her happiness at having saved the child's life. She and Cullen were all right, too, and a few aching fingers counted for little. She didn't have to worry about anyone recognizing her in Seattle, either. Wasn't that why she'd chosen this city?

"Are you all right?" she heard Cullen ask.

Her eyes flew open, and she nodded. "I didn't think we'd need this."

He shrugged. "We probably don't. But there's such a thing as liability, and they have to make sure we're fine."

She stared up at him, guilt suffusing her. "I haven't said thank you. You saved us. I'm not sure I would've been able to hang on to him in the water. . . ." She shrugged limply, not wanting to play those horrid thoughts in her mind. It scared her all over again to imagine it.

Cullen smiled slowly. "No need to thank me. You did all the hard stuff." He'd been damn sure he wouldn't reach her in time, and it had scared the hell out of him. He quashed that thought. He had reached her, and they were okay. He grinned. "That was some little guy. He was like greased lightning. Even at the far end of the dock, I could tell he was trouble. Some boys are like windup toys—they just keep on going." He shook his head. "You have quick reflexes, KT Wynter."

Krystal felt her body flush with pleasure, her aching fingers and strained arms and shoulders forgotten. "Thank you."

"I mean it. If you hadn't been sharp enough to figure out what was happening, he could've been gone. And it would've been hell trying to find him."

"Thank you." She shook her head. Why couldn't

she say something besides that? She felt so tongue-tied with Cullen Dempsey. "I just remembered when I used to take care of the children . . ." Her voice faded, and she looked away from him.

"You ran a day care center?" he asked swiftly, eager to get some personal information out of her. She'd halted as though she'd been about to blurt a state secret. Her reticence, her air of mystery, intrigued the hell out of him.

"Of sorts, yes," Krystal answered vaguely. Lancaster, Pennsylvania, and the children were light years away from Seattle. Another world. Another time. She'd been happy baby-sitting the farm children when their parents had worked in the fields. She'd been a Mennonite then, as had the children, and she'd laughed and played with them, and thought she'd be there forever. Now she could never go back.

"You look as though you regret telling me that," Cullen said. "Why?"

"I—I just don't like to talk about my life, Mr. Dempsey."

"Cullen. Call me that. I answer better."

"All right."

He noticed she didn't tell him to call her KT. He might anyway. "So you don't like to talk about your life? Good. I love to talk about mine. We'll make a pact. I'll talk, you listen."

"Fine." She smiled as some of the tension left her. He wasn't going to pry.

When the ambulance swayed around a corner, she felt his hand steady on her arm, its warmth penetrating through her clothes to her chilled skin. It somehow mitigated the icy dread that filled her as the near tragedy rose like a specter in her mind. It was over. He'd saved them. Still, she trembled.

The attendant moved toward her at once, adjusting a switch. "We have you on a heated mattress, ma'am. You should be very warm soon." He snapped the blood pressure band on her again, pumping it up a few times.

"And you're probably getting a reaction," Cullen said softly. "Even the best heroines get them." She was so vulnerable, he mused, so white-faced, so stiff. He had to stem the urge to pick her up and cradle her to him, warming her, letting her warm him.

"And she is a heroine," the attendant said, smiling widely.

"Yes, she is," Cullen whispered, his hand lifting of its own volition to stroke her face.

"Thank you," Krystal said once more, shivering at his touch. Why couldn't she find something else to say? Feeling as though she was both freezing and overheating, she stared up at him helplessly. Why did he have such an effect on her? He'd catapulted into her life, and instead of fading away, he stuck like a burr. He was annoying . . . but endearing. And because she did find him endearing, he was more threatening to her peace of mind than anything had been since her arrival in Seattle.

His kind tones were almost her undoing. She had such a need to cry . . . and she'd been dry-eyed for two years. She wanted to yield, bend, unwind, but her backbone had been poker-stiff for too long. She didn't dare give way, for fear the rest of her would collapse too. Maybe if she had stayed in San Francisco and outfaced them all, she wouldn't feel the need to hide from people. But it had all been so overwhelming at the time. She shook her head. She wouldn't conjure up those memories now. Whatever might have been was behind her, and she'd live with her decision. Running and hiding had been the viable way out at the time.

After one last turn, they were at the hospital, and then there were all sorts of people surrounding her.

The hospital was filled with badly hurt people. The doctors who attended to Cullen and Krystal were rushed, and happy to see patients who weren't so damaged. They were soon discharged.

Krystal dressed herself in dry, borrowed clothes, her hands fumbling over the fasteners, the slight shakiness in her limbs slowing her. She picked up her wet clothing, wrapped in plastic, and left the cubicle. She wasn't surprised to see Cullen waiting for her in the anteroom.

"Shall we go?" he said. "I've called a cab."

"Thanks." She only had to go a few short steps from the exit to the waiting vehicle, but it chilled her, and she huddled down into the warmth of the cab.

"You'd better get into a hot bath, then lie down for a while," Cullen said. "Might be a good idea to take the night off." He slid closer to her, putting his arm around her and easing her against him. "You've had a shock."

"I can't. I still have one person out with the flu. I have to fill in again." It stunned her, how good she felt being held by him. After no personal contact with any men for two years, the sensation of Cullen Dempsey's body pressed to hers was even more shocking than almost hurtling into Elliot Bay.

"Fine," he said. "I'll work late tonight and drive you home."

"There's no need. You'll be exhausted if you put in a full day, then wait for me." The idea of being driven home by Cullen Dempsey was more than just comforting. It was downright pleasing.

"Don't be silly. When I used to be out on the boats, we'd sometimes be up for twenty-four hours at a stretch. I've gotten used to long stints. Cat-napping's my secret." He grinned down at her. "Have dinner with me tomorrow night."

"What?" She stared at him as the world turned upside down.

"Don't look so stunned. It was a perfectly polite proposal. Dinner. You have to eat anyway. And you don't go to work until later."

"I'm . . . I don't usually work as late as I did the other night. We're often done an hour after midnight at the latest." Why was she explaining to him? she asked herself. He was nothing to her.

"All right," Cullen said. "We'll eat early, then I'll drive you home. You can change, gather your things, and I'll have you at work on time."

Rays of winter sunlight slashed into the cab, glinting over her features, delineating their seeming fragility, outlining those wonderful cheekbones, giving fire to her green eyes. Though she was so slender she looked as though she'd snap in a strong wind, he realized now that her insides were tough and caring and courageous. She had power, a quiet energy that emanated from her, baring a hidden sensuality. She was a real beauty, but it wasn't something you discovered right off. It just kind of whirled around her like an elusive aura, then would unexpectedly zap him. It was like her curly hair, which she'd bound down her back in a braid. But the wayward strands wouldn't be held down. They'd released themselves, framing her face and enticing him to run his fingers through them. He wanted to know more about KT Wynter. He wanted to know everything.

She drew in a deep breath, then exhaled it slowly. "All right," she said. "Dinner it is." She felt light-headed.

Cullen didn't realize he'd been holding his own breath until she answered. Air expelled from his lungs in a rush. "Good." He kept her close to his side as the cab wound its way toward her place. "Since our pact is that you listen and I talk, I expect you to hang on my every word," he said with mock solemnity. When he heard her breathy chuckle, his heart almost slammed through his chest. His reaction to her laughter surprised him as much as the laugh itself. He loved the sound of it. The woman had a strange effect on him. Why was he so pleased that he'd made her laugh?

"I'll wait with bated breath for each pearl," Krystal said, feeling an unaccustomed serenity sitting in the back of the dingy cab with Cullen, a lightness of spirit that had been missing from her life for some time.

"Good," he said. "Well, let's see. We might as well get started. First, I own my own business with a partner, so I'll be able to afford the hamburger and coffee I buy you for dinner."

"That's a relief." How long had it been since she'd bandied words with anyone? she wondered. That was easy. More than two years ago, when everything ended.

"But I might ask you to pay the tip," he added.

"Hah. I should have known. A catch." Cullen was fun, she mused, and very handsome. His face looked chiseled out of bronze, hard-planed, with eyes set wide apart. Actually, all of him looked carved from stone, but there was a gentleness about the big man. She could feel it.

"Not a catch, just a small hitch." She'd come alive, he thought. Her eyes glinted with humor, and her skin had taken on a luminescence. The beauty that he knew began deep in her soul radiated out of her.

She laughed, but then that happy sound faded away. He saw shadows drop over her face, as though someone had pulled a shade. Who'd hurt her and made it a sin to laugh? he wondered. Black memories had obviously blotted out her fun. And she was too young for that. He wanted to see that face of beauty lit with amusement all the time.

He walked her to the door of her building while the cab waited for him. He was about three hours late for a meeting. "Maybe I'll see you around the building," he said. "If not, I'll pick you up here at six sharp tomorrow. How's that?"

Krystal nodded, then watched him bound down the steps to the cab. He waved as the taxi pulled away, and she waved back.

For the rest of the day she did things in a daze.

She checked all of the equipment in her neatly packed carryall, shook out and pressed her coveralls, and castigated herself for being nine kinds of a fool. What had made her accept his dinner invitation? Insanity, that was what. She read for a time, watched television, but she couldn't have said later what she read or saw.

Finally it was time to go to work.

She didn't see him all during her shift, though she looked around more than once, sure she heard him behind her.

The next day, Krystal was certain she'd hear from him early in the day. She only went out once, to get her hair trimmed and to pick up some groceries. Not that her appetite was that good. She'd promised herself she'd stay healthy, though, so she ate a great deal of fruit and raw vegetables. On her return, she checked her answering machine. No message. She didn't know what he'd say if he called, but she'd been sure he would. He hadn't, though.

At five o'clock she showered, trying to still the nervous hammering of her heart.

"Stop it," she muttered to herself. "You're just going out to dinner. No strings, no hassles."

Oh, yeah? her inner voice said. Do you know this man? He could be a serial killer.

"Nonsense. He stuck his neck out for a child. That's enough recommendation."

Fool.

At one minute to six, she was sure he'd changed his mind. She didn't know whether to be annoyed or relieved. She was dressed in her best outfit, one of the few from her San Francisco days that she hadn't been able to part with. It was a timeless Chanel suit of a peach-colored wool with crystal buttons on the jacket. She wore matching crystal earrings, but no rings or other jewelry. Her hair was swept back in a chignon, severe and plain. Businesslike. That was the image she wanted to project.

When her apartment buzzer sounded at one minute after six, she jumped. Swallowing hard, she pressed the intercom button. "I'll be right down."

"Fine."

She locked her apartment and put the key in her black shoulder bag. It was genuine leather. She'd found it at the Salvation Army store, and it almost matched her black leather shoes with the two-inch heels. They were old but comfortable, and she'd polished them to a rich sheen. Throwing her only winter coat over her shoulders, a full-length camel hair coat that was six years old, she took deep breaths and descended.

On the first-floor landing, Cullen was lounging against the newel post. "I thought I'd meet you partway and walk you to the door," he told her solemnly.

She laughed, and much of her tension eased. He really was nice. "Thank you."

"Anyone every tell you you're very polite?"

"Yes, you have," she said. When he threw back his head and laughed, she couldn't stem her smile. When she saw his car, however, her smile wobbled. It wasn't new, but it was a Porsche. Last time he'd had a Jaguar. "Lovely car," she murmured. Fishing and car theft, she thought. Nice combination.

He nodded, smiling. "This one's mine. The Jag belongs to my partner. Porsches aren't the best car for maintenance, but I like it. When I was in the air force, I was stationed in Germany. I bought this car secondhand, and have enjoyed it ever since."

"Ah, I know. It belonged to a little old lady in Stuttgart who only drove it on Sundays," Krystal said, chuckling.

Her husky laugh sent shivers up Cullen's back. When he helped her into the car, he was still laughing, and goose bumps were still running up and down his spine.

Krystal's heart was pounding out of rhythm at the way his hand had lingered at her waist. It was silly, she told herself. She was acting as if this were her first date.

The car was small, but comfortable, and she felt shut away from the world, encased in leather and steel. When Cullen slid behind the wheel and closed his door, it was as though the oxygen supply had been cut in half. She found herself slightly breathless. She inhaled deeply, but couldn't seem to fill her lungs. Her hand scrambled for the door latch, and only with great effort of will did she not open it. Instead she sat back, fastened her safety belt, and watched his long fingers fiddle with the instruments.

The car fired with a roar.

Cullen turned to smile at her before pulling away from the curb. "Nice evening." She nodded and looked out her window. He glanced at her thick hair, twisted into a tight knot at the back of her head. It was a sin not to let that wonderful hair hang free, he thought. What would it feel like to run his fingers through it? Damn. He was getting fanciful.

He pressed a button and a tape began to play, the music pure, pulsating, the dancing beat filling the car. He looked over at her again as he steered effortlessly through the slushy, snow-edged streets. She was sitting poker-stiff, as though he'd just made an indecent suggestion. "I think you'll like Angelique's. The food is good." He wanted her to relax, to enjoy, just as he wanted to do.

"I've heard of it. The hamburgers come with onion," she said, tongue in cheek.

He started, then chuckled. "Why do you keep that wonderful sense of humor locked away, KT Wynter? It's wild, sharp, and I love it." And he'd discovered something else. Being so close to her in the car was very arousing. He could feel desire throb to life, and it irked him—just a little—that she could have that kind of power over him without so much as the smallest come-on. He hadn't been this intrigued for many years.

His ego was balanced enough to know that women liked him and often sought his company. He had a normal sex drive and a healthy respect for women—and he liked them too. Women who were intellectual and cultured, had high-powered jobs, and possessed good self-esteem had always drawn him. What in hell had drawn him to KT Wynter, who seemed to have few of the traits he'd always thought he admired?

Krystal didn't notice the intent and curious glances Cullen was shooting at her, because she was mulling over his comment about her sense of humor.

"I don't hide my humor," she said at last. In fact, she never tried to mask it. It had been her fun, to see the bizarre in things, the twists and turns, rather than the straight. But, she realized now, her self-imposed isolation had all but blunted its spontaneity. What was it about Cullen that brought it back to life? "Sometimes I say crazy things," she added lamely.

"Care to tell me why?" he asked.

"No."

He shrugged at her blunt answer. "Okay. After all, the agreement was that I'd do the talking and you'd listen."

"Right." Relief flooded her. Again he'd surprised her by not pressing, not insisting.

They were silent for the rest of the short journey. Angelique's was on the first floor of a yellow brick building that looking like it had been built when Seattle was first settled.

"Like it?" Cullen asked as he stopped the car. He turned toward her, one eye on the approaching parking valet.

"Yes. It's lovely. It looks like a club."

The valet reached them and leaned down, smiling through the closed window on the passenger side.

Cullen ignored him. KT was getting uptight again. He could tell from the way she threaded her hands together. He took her left hand and clasped it tightly, hoping to put her at ease. "The valet looks tough," he said, lying shamelessly about the innocuous person waiting patiently under the marquee. "I'm hoping this is going to be an enjoy-able evening, but if anyone gives us any trouble, you hit low, I'll go high. We're a good team in a crunch."

Her head swung to him. "You're a nut," she said softly.

He nodded. "But we're such a great twosome, I thought you might overlook that."

"Are we?"

"We are. Shall we go?" He touched the button that unlocked the doors, then got out and walked swiftly around the car, helping her out before the valet could. "Ready?" he asked. She was white-faced. What did she think was ahead of her? he wondered. Who in hell had done such a job on her?

"Here's your ticket, sir."

Cullen scowled at the valet for shattering some of the fragile intimacy they'd built in the car. Sighing regretfully, he pocketed the ticket and took KT's arm.

"He thinks he just made an enemy," she said dryly. "Are your killing looks a specialty?"

"No, but I'm thinking about refining them into one." When she grinned, he almost fell over, his heart nose-diving with delight. He'd never seen such innocent sensuality, and his blood pounded hard. "As an afterthought," he said casually, trying to force his pulse back into normal rhythm, "did you know you're beautiful?" When she stiffened, looking alarmed, he put his arm around her. "That's a compliment, not an insult, KT. Please take it as such." Her slow nod had him exhaling in relief. She hadn't reerected all the barriers.

"I've been here twice before," he went on as the

maitre d' led them to their table. "The food is so good, I can't resist it."

Krystal looked around when she was seated, delighted with the table he'd chosen. It had privacy, yet she was able to see most of the other diners without their staring back at her. "Do you always demand the best table in the house?"

Cullen shrugged, pleased that she liked it. "Only if I'm dining with the city's prettiest woman," he said. He noted how her smile flagged, how her shoulders stiffened. The look she gave him was plastic, polite.

"I meant that," he said simply.

She looked disbelieving, but then credulity spread slowly across her face, bringing with it a shyness, a fluttering unsureness. Damn, he thought. She should expect such compliments, not question them.

A minute passed in silence, and he had the sense she was waging some sort of internal battle. Apparently, the good guys won, for she straightened in her chair and gazed directly at him, smiling slightly. The glitter of her beauty started with that smile and worked its way to her eyes, radiating out like her own personal beacon.

"I don't know what caused the metamorphosis, but I like it," he murmured, leaning forward. "You are lovely."

"You speak your mind," she said softly. "You'd be a marvelous diplomat. War would be declared every other day."

He chuckled. "Lady, you malign me."

She shook her head. "I'm truthful."

They concentrated on their menus then. After

the waiter had taken their order, Cullen surprised Krystal by standing and holding his hand out to her. She looked up at him mutely.

"I don't think we should waste the music," he said. "Shall we dance?"

She was out of her chair and preceding him to the dance floor before she realized it would've been better to have made an excuse.

A soft rock song was playing, the rhythm pulsing lightly through her as she stepped into Cullen's arms.

They moved together smoothly, and after a minute, she began to relax.

She'd forgotten how much she liked to dance. Cullen made it easy, beautiful, memorable. No one had ever done that to her on a dance floor, or off. And she wanted it so much, she closed her mind to the inner voices that warned her to be prudent. She felt as though the beat of the music was in her blood, as if her veins and arteries were in tune with Cullen Dempsey. It was magical, wonderful, and if she never experienced it again, at least she had it now.

One song followed another. Their bodies melded in rhythm.

Cullen had wanted other women before, and he'd had them. But never had the desire been matched by a need to cherish. He wanted KT, and he wanted to take care of her. That shook him.

Only when they saw the waiter hovering at their table did they reluctantly move apart and head to the table.

As she walked, Krystal's blood was still thrumming through her veins. Her head was filled with tiny flashing lights. Everything around her looked good, not threatening. She was happy with Cullen Dempsey! She wanted the evening to be everlasting.

Cullen was so damned aroused, he was annoyed with himself. He'd always been in control of his feelings for women. It had left him independent and still friends with the women he'd known. Now he was unsure. Being with KT was like holding a hot coal. He couldn't sustain the touch, yet he couldn't let go.

As he helped her into her chair, he leaned down and kissed the top of her head. "You're a wonderful dancer, KT." Her glowing smile and whispered thanks almost buckled his knees.

The food was choice—Pacific salmon with a sauce so light, it could have floated. With it they had a Caesar salad, with the anchovies, and crusty sourdough bread, hot and fragrant.

They lingered over the meal, smiling at each other, savoring the moment and their light conversation.

Not all of Krystal's many warnings to herself could prevent the warmth from seeping through her. Satisfaction was a woolen shawl wrapped tightly around the shoulders, keeping out the winter blasts.

"Sometime I'll take you out on one of the boats," Cullen said impulsively.

She nodded, smiling, not letting the bogeys change her mind. There might not be any other times with Cullen. Prudence dictated that she avoid any other meetings. But why rock the boat of a beautiful evening with negatives? Tomorrow could take care of itself.

Reason told her the service was superb, the food delicious. Yet she was unaware of everything but Cullen. One forkful followed another, inanities flowed back and forth, but there was a silence to sound, a muteness to speech. Only the eyes told the truth of the fire building between them.

Krystal was titillated, overwhelmed, laughing, joyous . . . but fearful.

Cullen was surprised, intrigued, delighted . . . and determined to see her again.

They danced once more. All too soon it was time to go.

Krystal couldn't believe the wrenching regret she felt as they left the private world they'd created at Angelique's.

Cullen felt deprived. He had to take her home and he didn't want that. Already he felt he'd lost her. Threading his fingers with hers, he led her out into the crisp yet misty-cold Seattle night. "Beautiful," he whispered, looking at her.

"Lovely," she answered, recalling their oneness on the dance floor.

People rushed by them, huddled in their coats, faces screwed up against the biting breeze. Krystal and Cullen looked up and inhaled deeply.

"The best time to take a stroll," Krystal murmured. When she slipped a bit on the ice and he tightened his grip, she curled her fingers around his, feeling the heat of his touch suffuse her. "I enjoyed myself," she said abruptly, glad and appalled she'd admitted so much. She wanted to tell him she hadn't had such a good time since she'd left Pennsylvania, but she added nothing more.

A hot tide of pleasure shook Cullen, and surprise followed in its wake. He was like a schoolboy with her. Her words had made him vibrate with joy.

"I enjoyed myself too," he said. He tugged on her hand, just a little, bringing her into his side, so that when they walked, they bumped each other. "I'd like to do it again." When she hesitated, he cursed his gaucherie. He was rushing her. He knew she was shy, extremely reticent. Hold back, he told himself. Don't push.

She drew in a deep breath and looked up at him. She bit her lip, then said, "So would I."

He stopped and tugged her around to face him, staring down at her intently. The streetlight streaked her face with silver, but he knew she was blushing at his long look. He threw back his head and laughed out loud, then lifted her, swinging her around until she was laughing, too, and passersby were either grinning or frowning at them. At last he set her on her feet and hugged her. "Tomorrow?"

She nodded, her head against his shoulder.

He leaned back so he could see her face. "I won't let you change your mind."

"I won't," she said huskily. When she saw his mouth descending, her first instinct was to turn away. A better reaction had her reaching up to bring him down to her.

The kiss was gentle, warm, wanting. Hearts beat in racing crescendo. Blood simmered hotly. Awareness was full-blown. This was no casual moment.

They pulled back at the same time, eyeing each other warily.

Krystal couldn't prevent the shiver of certainty that ran through her. She wanted to be with him, to tell him who she was, why she was in Seattle. She wanted Cullen Dempsey to stay in Seattle, too, near her.

He felt her tremor. "You're cold." He kissed her forehead, then wrapped his arm around her. "Let's go back and get the car." He wasn't cold, not with a volcano of passion erupting within him. KT sometimes made him feel like he was walking on a waxed tightrope, but he wanted it, and was willing to risk his fear of heights to stay with her.

The valet brought the car around in record time, and this time they frowned at him for unwittingly hurrying the end of their evening.

Within a minute they were driving down the street. For the first time in his life, Cullen wished for a blowout. Running out of gas might be a little suspect.

Krystal had her own wishes. She wanted to tell Cullen about San Francisco, and about growing up in a Mennonite community in Lancaster, Pennsylvania, with loving, hardworking people who'd been like a cocoon around her. It had ended when her mother, who had been raised in that community, died, and her father, who'd always been an outsider, had returned after several years absence to take her away. They'd led a gypsylike existence until she was almost twenty. Finally, they'd settled in San Francisco. Her father had started a business and married again. She'd gotten a step-mother, one she loved, revered—

Krystal couldn't go on with the thoughts. They stung like barbs under her skin. If only she could talk about it to Cullen. . . .

"Here we are," he said gloomily as he stopped in front of her home. He got out of the car and walked around to her side. Opening her door, he frowned at her. "I didn't want this evening to end."

She laughed. "You read my mind." Then she caught her breath as he reached in the car and all but lifted her to the sidewalk.

He kept his arm around her as they walked up to the door. Then he leaned down and kissed her cheek. "Let me see you upstairs. I'd feel better. Then I'll go."

She didn't want him to go. That thought rattled her so much, her hand shook and she could barely unlock her door. Then she was leading him up the stairs, hotly aware that he was right at her heels. "I've made an offer on a new place," she said abruptly, nervously. "I'll have just one flight of stairs to climb there."

"I'll help you move." A chance to be with her all day!

She turned to face him at her door. "Thank you." She held out her hand, drew it back, put it out again. When he slid his arms around her and kissed her gently, she melted against him, her hands lightly touching his waist.

"Good night," he murmured. "I'll call you tomorrow." He smiled at her, then turned and went down the stairs two at a time.

Krystal entered her apartment, her fingers pressed to her lips as though she could hold the kiss there forever. Cullen Dempsey! He'd torn into her life like a jackhammer ripping through concrete. And she was walking on air!

Three

Three weeks later was moving day. Krystal stood in the shambles of her old apartment, her thoughts on Cullen instead of her packing. He'd been with her since early morning. At that moment he was at her new place overseeing the setting up of her office. Soon he'd be back. Her heart tripped like a child skipping rope. She giggled out loud as she wrapped her few dishes in newspaper.

"D'ja say some'pn, lady?"

"Ah, no." She smiled lamely at the mover, who was squinting at her questioningly. "That box goes next. I'll follow along in my van with those in the corner."

She couldn't tell the man she'd been daydreaming about the dinner she'd had with Cullen the night before, about their trip to the market to find just the right salmon, which they'd grilled on the tiny fire-escape landing just outside her kitchen window. Since the two of them couldn't be on the rickety structure at the same time, they'd kept the window open so they could converse. Then they'd had to don their coats to eat because the apartment had gotten too cold. The night had been magical! She hadn't known there could be such wonderful happenings between men and women.

She laughed out loud, then sobered as the mover stomped back into the room.

"That's it, lady." he said, giving her a strange look. "We'll meet you at the new place. I got the key."

She nodded, biting her lip to keep from laughing again. He thought her crazy. And she was, she mused as the man left. Crazy for letting Cullen Dempsey so far inside her life. Now he was entrenched, and she was delighted and terrified.

Their first few dates had turned into daily contact. All her steadfast plans to stay in isolation had gone up in smoke. She'd begun listening to the inner voice that had questioned the wisdom of her actions for the past two years, that had told her she was foolish to hide away. Now, she wondered. Maybe she should have stayed in San Francisco, faced the unpleasantness. One way or another, she'd be in the open. Since meeting Cullen, being open had taken on new meaning. She wanted it in her life.

More than once, in the past few weeks, when she'd been washing a floor, or dusting and polishing furniture, she'd asked herself if it wouldn't have been easier to face down her critics from the start, taken the hit, then gotten back up and struggled to keep going.

Now, to add to her growing disquiet, there was

Cullen Dempsey. And he was becoming more insistent than her other, negative inner voice. She wanted his company, the touch of life he was offering her, his exuberance, and laughter.

She glanced at her watch. He should be back soon. Then they'd cart the rest of her things to the van, and they'd drive to her new home together. Her heart pounded heavily. She missed him, she wanted him there beside her.

And he was.

"Hi," he said, strolling into the room. He walked right over to her, bent down, and kissed her deeply.

"Hi," she said breathlessly. The wonder of him silenced the warning voice inside that urged her to go slow.

Cullen stared at her and thought her beautiful, with her dirt-smudged nose and shabby smock. "You're gorgeous."

She laughed. "You're crazy."

"Yeah. I told you we're a team."

"So you did." She closed her eyes when he kissed her again, and she didn't hear the prudent admonitions being voiced in her very core. All she heard was music, joy . . . love. Cullen did that to her.

Krystal was in her new office one afternoon a week later when her phone rang. She knew who it was before she said hello.

After asking how she was settling into her new home, Cullen asked if she was working that evening. She told him she wasn't.

"Good," he said, then chuckled. "I can remember

rushing to get a date home before curfew so I wouldn't be in trouble with her father, but getting her home so she won't be late for work is a new one."

"No more of that for a while. I have a full staff at last," she said happily. Now all she had to do was keep the books, pay the money, and supervise the jobs. That didn't take the long hours she had to put in when doubling for a worker. Everything was back to normal, until the next crisis. She'd even gone shopping that afternoon. She'd bought a pair of panty hose and felt as though she'd purchased an entire new wardrobe.

"I have a special place to take you tonight, KT Wynter."

"You do every night."

"Well, you're a special lady." He paused. "It'll be different tomorrow night. I hope you'll be free, then, too."

"I will. Why the difference?"

"It's more involved." And they wouldn't be alone, Cullen added silently, as they usually were. He regretted that. His dinners with KT had been wonderful. They'd talked and talked. She still hadn't opened up to him, although he'd told her everything. And she could discuss a variety of subjects with him, ranging from politics to art history. She intrigued him more each time he saw her. That was why tomorrow was going to be a little bit of a surprise. He had to have some secrets. He smiled as he thought that. He was like a kid with her.

Her voice interrupted his musings. "You've been taking me to special places every night, Cullen. I hope none of this has been on an expense account, because your partner will be questioning all these extravagances."

"None. You're definitely not business, KT. You're strictly pleasure." He heard the quick intake of her breath, and knew he'd made another blunder. Not for the first time, he wanted to demand she tell him everything. It was like skating on thin ice to talk with her. He'd misspoken so many times, yet he didn't know why. "Speaking of him—my partner, that is—he'll be meeting us for dinner tomorrow night." He decided it would be better to warn her after all rather than surprise her. KT could be edgy at times.

Krystal's usual wariness was accompanied by an alien rush of disappointment. She and Cullen had been alone for three weeks, and it had been wonderful. She'd begun to look forward to those long, drugging good-night kisses that left her weak and wanting more. Nothing in her life had prepared her for Cullen Dempsey. Wild storm's of emotion, oceans of feelings hitherto unplumbed. Those wonderful kisses that were eroding her control, her restraint, her caution, and making her ache for more, pine for the man. More than once she'd almost urged him to join her in her apartment, but she'd refrained. She wasn't yet ready to risk the pain again.

"Is this going to be dressy?" she asked prudently.

"Some get very dressed up, some are more casual. You always look right."

She went weak at the huskiness in his voice, at the hopeful tone. But it didn't soothe her. A formal evening. Lord! She wanted to look right for Cullen. And she didn't want to be fearful.

Cullen knew by her silence that she was wrestling with what he'd said, that she wasn't sure she should go. "I'm supposed to go," he added, then decided to throw down the gauntlet, bare his soul. "And I'd like you with me."

"Dressy," she said limply, running her meager wardrobe around in her head.

"Dressy, but street-length is fine." She hadn't said no! He wanted to jump right through the phone, take her in his arms, and soothe away her trepidation. He'd seen her every night for three weeks, sometimes for not more than an hour, but they'd been together. At first, when he'd kissed her good night, it had only been a light kiss or two on her lips. Yet those brief caresses had driven him wild. He hadn't been able to work an hour straight without thinking of her. The past couple of evenings, the kisses had been the most erotic he'd ever experienced, and he wanted more. He wanted her. He sensed she wanted him, too, but she was battling it every step of the way.

"So," she said, "tell me more about tomorrow night."

He heard a note of uneasiness in her voice, different from the wariness he'd grown accustomed to. "What's wrong, KT?" he asked quietly.

When she didn't speak for a moment, he thought she wasn't going to answer. Then she blurted out, "You're very good to me. Why?"

He frowned. Did she find what he did for her so incredible? "I'm good to me too. I like being with you. You're beautiful, witty, and intelligent. What man wouldn't want to be with a woman like you?"

She was silent again for a long moment. "Why are you bothering?" she finally asked, and it was as though the words had been pulled from her, as if this was something she had to know, even if it were distasteful.

He brought the phone close to his mouth. "How do I know? Maybe because I have a thing for janitors."

Laughter burst from her. "That must be it."

"Keep that thought."

"I will," Krystal said softly, her insides fluttering like butterfly wings. When she hung up, she put her head in her hands for a few minutes, her thoughts chaotic, her whole being in upheaval. Where was she going with him tomorrow night? Why had she agreed without questioning? She was crazy, but . . . no matter. She was going with him! She'd battle down any argument against that, because she wanted it so much. Being with Cullen had cracked her barriers, made her wonder about the wisdom—or foolishness—of the course she'd taken when she'd first run to Seattle. After all, she'd really done nothing wrong in San Francisco. Did it matter how others perceived her?

Now wasn't the time to ask that question, though. It should have come two years ago. No, she'd gone too far to go back and she'd hurt people she loved. So, she was set on a course . . . but she was veering off for a little while, to be with Cullen Dempsey.

Refusing to think about it any longer, she rose and went to the closet, fingering the few good clothes hanging there.

• • •

The next night Cullen arrived early and raced up to the second floor.

She opened the door at the first knock, smiling at him. "I saw you arrive from my window. I don't know how you can run up those stairs . . . What is it?" He looked pale all at once, stricken. "Are you in pain? You shouldn't have run that way." She reached out and took his arm, pulling him into the apartment. "Come and sit down, Cullen."

"I'm out of breath because of you, not because I ran up the stairs," he said abruptly, turning her around to face him. "You knock me out, lady. You look like a rose—velvety, warm, and desirable." He touched the sleeve of her satin suit. "What color do they call this? Sunshine?"

"I call it lemon," she said huskily.

"You look good enough to eat. Not like a lemon, though. More like a luscious apricot. I love eating fruit." She reddened, and he smiled. He hadn't intended the double entendre. It wasn't his style, but he wouldn't call it back, either. He'd meant every word. "I've never seen more beautiful skin than yours, KT." He leaned down and kissed her cheek, letting his mouth linger there. He wished he could put diamonds on her ears and on her fingers, instead of the simple gold earrings she wore. He wanted to give her anything she craved. He wanted to give her the world.

"Would you like a drink?" Krystal asked, hoping to distract him. His hot, probing look seemed to enter her body, firing her blood. She needed something to do with her nervous and jerky hands, and making a drink seemed a reasonable option. Not that she had a large bar selection. She didn't. She hadn't even had a glass of wine since her arrival in Seattle. On her best days she'd never been much of a tippler, but after the fiasco in San Francisco, she'd forsworn taking even a drop of alcohol. It was strange, she mused, the way San Francisco and her father could pop into her mind, even when she only wanted to concentrate on Cullen.

She was preoccupied again, Cullen thought, seeing bleak memories shadow her eyes once more. She'd often slip away from him that way. Maybe one day she'd tell him about what cocooned her at times. "No," he said. "We should go. We only have a little over an hour before dinner." He gazed at her regretfully. "I'd rather stay here."

The slumbrous look in his eyes sent her pulse racing as panic and excitement rose in her. She wouldn't think of yesterdays, she told herself, or dwell on anything that would make her pull back from Cullen. "I'd rather stay, too," she said, "but . . . we should go." In her eagerness to leave, she forgot to ask him their destination.

When they were in his car, Cullen turned to her. "This dinner is to honor my partner, by the way. He's quite a man." He kissed her nose, then sat back and stared at her. As her gaze locked with his, she saw the now-familiar desire darken his eyes. He leaned across the console once more and placed his lips on hers, not pressing or opening his mouth.

She had the distinct feeling he was requesting permission. Heat suffused her, and she moved closer, slanting her mouth beneath his, her lips parting easily.

When he felt the first touch of her tongue, Cullen's heart slammed against his chest, his muscles convulsing reflexively, his skin goose-bumping. God, he wanted her. He lifted his mouth a fraction. "KT," he murmured, stroking her cheek with one finger.

She saw the question in his eyes. "We have to go," she said huskily, regretfully. "You said it was important."

"It is," he said hoarsely. "But so is this."

She nodded, because she had to be truthful with him, because she wanted that between them. She put her hand on his chest, feeling his thudding heart, whose rhythm matched hers. "There's time."

"There has to be," he muttered, and kissed her again, hard, letting her feel his need. Releasing her, he leaned back in his seat, staring at her, feeling they'd traveled a thousand miles in those few precious minutes. "We've crossed a chasm, KT. No going back."

"No going back," she repeated.

As they drove, Cullen reached for and held her hand each time he finished shifting. They said little, and much of it was just polite inanities. Words meant nothing. Breathing, tones, body movements, were all. He felt her stiffen when he turned into the drive of the private airfield.

"We're flying?" she asked.

"Are you afraid to fly?"

"No. Actually, I like it." She stared at a small jet, poised on the runway, as he parked the car. "No wonder you didn't think we'd have enough time, even though we had more than an hour."

"And now we have to hurry." He caught her hand and ran for the jet.

Out of breath and laughing, she turned to look at him as they ran. "Are you a pilot?"

"Yes." They stopped in front of the shallow steps, and he swept her up into his arms and lifted her into the cabin.

Grabbing hold of the door, she turned to him as he climbed in behind her. "For a fisherman, you're pretty versatile," she said.

"I'm glad you noticed." Laughing, he ushered her into the cockpit, taking the left seat and gesturing that she take the other.

He leaned over and kissed her on the nose when she sat and stared at him wide-eyed. "Strap in, sweet one," he said. "We're ready for takeoff." He felt buoyant, alive. He didn't want to question why being with KT meant so much to him. All he did know was that she made him happy. He contacted the tower, listened to the instructions, and smiled at her.

Before Krystal had time to wonder if she was ready, they were in the air. "I can't believe we're doing this, but I like it." After two years of incessant hard work, she was soaring, both physically and spiritually, over beautiful Washington. They circled Seattle and headed south, but not before she'd taken a good hard look at Mt. Rainier. It was wonderful, and even more beautiful from the air.

When she laughed, Cullen felt his heart swell with delight. Pleasing her made him more pleased than he could ever remember being.

He put on music, then radioed ahead to make sure a car would be waiting. " We're cutting it fine, KT, but we should be there in less time than I figured. Good tail wind."

She nodded, replaying the bits of his conversation with the tower that she'd heard. Had he said they were flying to Los Angeles? That would be fine, but it was pretty far. Could they get there in time? It didn't matter, she thought, just as long as she was with Cullen.

She settled back and watched everything, but especially his strong, sure hands as they moved confidently over the controls. The plane seemed to sing through the clouds, and she drank it all in. If they didn't do anything else that evening, if they took off again immediately after landing, the evening would be a dream come true. Flying was freedom!

"You're enjoying it, aren't you, KT?"

She nodded, not wanting to speak and break the spell of being in the cabin with Cullen, listening to soft music, and feeling more secure than she'd ever felt before.

In less time than she would've figured, they were descending. It was then, as she looked at the approaching ground, speeding up to meet them, that familiar landmarks registered in her mind. She began to perspire; her hands shook. San Francisco! Heaven help her. Why hadn't she made him tell her their destination, instead of acting like a moonstruck teenager on her first date? Quick glances at Cullen showed he hadn't seen her agitation. Totally absorbed in getting landing instructions from the tower and in positioning the aircraft for landing, he hadn't looked her way since beginning descent. Go back! she cried silently. Go back!

Then they were on the ground, zinging down a runway and taxiing to a stop in front of a large hangar. People walked out toward the plane, some looking up and waving to Cullen. He waved back, smiling.

When he turned to KT, his smile faded instantly at the sight of her white face. "Did the landing frighten you?" He took her hand. It was downright clammy.

She gazed down at their entwined hands. "Must have," she mumbled.

He leaned over and unbuckled her, kissing her cheek. "Sorry. I wasn't thinking. I love flying so much, I forget that other people don't. Come on, we'll get some food and something cool to drink, then you'll feel better."

"Of course."

But how was she to feel better being back in the city where her father had died and where her step-mother still lived? But San Francisco was a big city, she told herself. She wouldn't see her step-mother. And they were returning to Seattle that evening. Guilt assailed her as she thought of the woman who'd been so close to her, the woman she had thought had betrayed her, the woman who was as alone in the world as she. She shook her head to clear her jumbled thoughts. Perhaps one day she could call her stepmother; maybe even see her. What had happened two years ago didn't loom as large in her mind anymore, thanks to Cullen. She knew she'd blown it out of proportion to an extent, and that she might have blamed the blameless.

She followed Cullen out of the cockpit. He went down the steps of the plane first, then turned and lifted her down.

"Relax, KT," he said, holding her close. "We're going to have a great evening." He led her toward a rented car, his arm around her shoulder.

She nodded, almost afraid to speak. Where were they going for dinner? she wondered.

"You'll like The Ballroom," he said, as if he'd read her mind. "It's near the Embarcadero. And they have a chef who specializes in Italian food."

She'd never heard of The Ballroom, she thought with relief. It wasn't a place she'd ever partied at with her father or stepmother. "Italian food can be very special in San Francisco," she said, and tried to smile, even though she knew it was a poor effort.

Sitting in the passenger seat of the plush Cadillac Seville that carried them toward the Embarcadero, she gazed raptly at the city that she'd once thought was the most wonderful place she'd ever seen. And for a few years, it had been.

"You're very quiet," Cullen said, wondering why her color hadn't come back. Could it have been the flying? He shouldn't have tried to surprise her.

"I'm just looking at the city. It's quite attractive, isn't it?"

"Yes." He wasn't fooled. Something was eating at her.

"Oh, I think you missed your turn if you want the square," she said. "Now you'll have to go up three blocks and cut back." She gasped in obvious dismay at her own words and sat back.

"Right." He shot her a quick glance. "Sounds like you know the city pretty well."

"I—I do. Not like a native, but I did live here for three years." Two lifetimes ago, she thought, in a setting of macabre clowns. A black comedy in which no one was a winner. Especially her father, who'd killed himself rather than stand trial for fraud.

"How long ago?" Cullen asked, trying to stifle his eagerness at this bit of personal information she was finally giving him.

"I left over two years ago," she said. "I haven't been back since, but . . ." Her voice faded, and she was silent for a minute. "I might come back again soon and visit," she said suddenly.

He eyed her again, almost a little too long. When he glanced back at the road, he quickly had to correct his direction as the big car veered and caused a cacophony of honking. At least KT's color was coming back, he thought. Whatever decision she'd just made, it was apparently a good one. He reached out a hand and covered hers.

She curled her fingers around his. "Has anyone ever told you that you're a terrible driver?"

"Certainly not. That little lapse back there was undoubtedly a skid." He was relieved at her change of expression, the release of tension.

"On a dry road? No policeman would accept it." She smiled with genuine pleasure, enjoying the bantering. She had every right to be in San Francisco, she told herself with great assurance. She hadn't committed a crime. She'd been foolish, gullible. That was bad enough, but it wasn't illegal.

"And are you going to call a policeman?" he asked.

"Maybe."

"KT, you're a traitor."

She laughed and leaned her head back, sighing as she closed her eyes. It could be a very nice evening. If she couldn't completely oust the churning gremlins from her innards, at least she could redefine them and deal with them. It didn't cost that much to be sensible, and that's what she would be. She would handle whatever came along, this evening and any other.

Cullen glanced over at KT constantly, watching the silvery play of city lights over her lovely face. She had the appearance of fragility, as tough she'd break with the slightest pressure. But under that translucent skin beat strength and determination. She was making a go of a tough business. He could identify with that. But there was also an elusive innocence about her. He wanted to know it all, and she'd at last given him an opening.

When Cullen drove into an underground parking lot, Krystal opened her eyes. The garage looked familiar, but then, she thought, all parking garages look alike.

He parked the car and turned to her. "Since you like to dance, how about if we do just that before we fly home?"

She recalled the many nights in San Francisco when she'd danced until dawn. She nodded slowly. "I'd like that very much."

"Great." He grinned at her, then got out and

walked around to her side of the car. "Let's go. My feet are itching."

"Try antibiotic cream."

He pulled her from the car and into his arms, laughing. "Irreverent brat," he said, his mouth pressed against her hair. He drew back and gazed into her eyes. "You're beautiful and you have a marvelous sense of humor, and the most wonderful green eyes." He kissed her lightly on the lips, then tugged her closer, his mouth slanting across hers, the kiss deepening.

Bells, horns, and whistles went off in her head. She barely heard the catcall from someone passing. She pulled back, her hands splayed against his chest, out of breath and trembling. "People," she gasped.

Confused, befuddled, Cullen stared down at her. "Where?"

"Here. In the garage. All around us." She stared up at him. In the bronzy garage light, he looked hewn from that metal. At that moment she wanted him with more than desire. She wanted his mind and spirit. It shook her that she'd let go of her emotions so much, they'd twined around Cullen and tied her to him.

"You're beautiful," he said huskily. "We should go." He didn't move.

"I thought we were going to dance," she said breathily.

"Uh-huh." He wanted to stay where they were, not moving. Holding her gave him a delight he'd never known. "I want you, lady. Is it too soon to tell you?"

Struck dumb for a moment, she shook her head.

"Good. We'll talk about it later." He kissed her cheek, knowing his easy tone hadn't entirely masked his heart beating out of rhythm, his blood pulsing so hard, he felt dizzy. He pulled her hand through his arm and threaded his fingers with hers. He wanted her badly, and in more ways than he'd wanted any other woman. He wanted to give everything to KT . . . and he wanted everything in return.

They didn't look at each other as they walked to the elevator, but awareness palpitated through them and around them like an electrical cable knocked down and blowing wildly in a storm. Charges shot all over the place. Power crackled in an aura that only they could feel. It was enervating, and at the same time more energizing than anything they'd ever experienced.

"It looks like a crowd will be here," Krystal said idly, gazing at the throng of cars clustered together. Her knees felt like they would melt and spill her all over the floor. "Most of them must be here for the event we're attending," she added. She didn't know that! But what did it matter anyway? Her mind wouldn't settle on anything. She was a caldron of sensation, and nothing more. And Cullen was at the center of it.

When they stepped into the elevator, Cullen hauled her into his arms. "No one here," he whispered, not sure he could explain even to himself his need for her.

"Right. My lip gloss will be gone when we arrive." She didn't care two pins for that.

"I'll try to give you time to repair it," he said thickly.

"Fair enough," she said. She threaded her hands

through his hair. "You might be a little messed up too."

"I'll risk it," he murmured, his mouth centimeters from hers. He kissed her then, his lips parting over hers, his heart pounding out of rhythm.

They clung to each other, as though when the elevator doors opened they'd be separated forever.

Cullen couldn't get a handle on his feelings. He couldn't even reach them. They were out of sight, out of mind. They were chaotic, and more turbulent than anything he'd ever experienced.

Once when diving in the shark-infested waters off Australia, he and some companions had come face-to-face with a great white shark. Angered by their invasion of his territory, the shark had attacked with the single-mindedness of a dedicated killer. There were many divers and they'd fought back and killed the beast, but not before several of them were wounded, two severely. Cullen had never forgotten the whirling, whorling caldron the sea had become as they'd battled the undersea carnivore. He'd never thought he'd again experience anything akin to it. Yet KT whirled him to the depths of all the seas, then spun him up through the water, up, up, beyond the earth to the firmament. At that moment he was one with her, melded to her in a way words couldn't express. He was KT's now and a hundred years henceforth.

Tightening his hold, he deepened the kiss, letting her know his passion, his commitment to her, and his desire to have her want him as much.

Krystal kissed Cullen with all the verve and passion she'd denied for over two years. The shell that had enclosed her for so long cracked, splintered, shattered about her feet. She leaned against his body, sighing her passion into his mouth as he whirled her away in a hurricane of sensations unlike any she'd ever known.

The elevator doors opened.

Krystal heard a sudden silence, then laughter. Fuzzily she surfaced from the passion-induced vortex and glimpsed several people out of the corner of her eye. She and Cullen were the focus of their laughter! She tried to pull back, even as her spirit seemed still linked to Cullen.

"We're—we're here," she stammered.

"Where?" Cullen stared at her dazedly. A bright light surrounded them, enclosing them. Why the hell had she pulled back? Dammit, he'd been loving her. And who the hell was laughing?

"You're at my party," he heard Gadsden say. Chuckling, the older man reached through the closing elevator doors and yanked on his partner, getting him and his new friend out of the elevator. "Where did you think?"

"Heaven," Cullen muttered for KT's ears only.

"How do you do?" Gadsden said to her. "I'm Gadsden Worth, Cullen's partner. And you must be KT."

"Yes." Still shaken, Krystal couldn't look at him or any of the other avidly interested guests. Her face heating with embarrassment at all the assessing stares, she faced Gadsden, her smile strained. "Perhaps I could freshen up."

"Of course, my dear," Gadsden said kindly. "Just up the stairs and to the left. An attendant will show you."

"Thank you." A final shred of dignity was the

only thing that kept her from pressing the button for the elevator again and escaping. She pushed back from Cullen, and he let her go reluctantly.

"She's quite lovely," Gadsden said to Cullen as KT ascended the stairs. "I like your new friend."

"So do I," Cullen answered, still staring at KT.

Gadsden chuckled. "I can see that. What's her full name?"

"KT Wynter," Cullen replied absently, not taking his eyes off her until she disappeared from sight, not seeing the surprise on his friend's face when he mentioned her name.

"Wynter," Gadsden repeated with surprise. "I wonder if she's any relation to Violet Wynter. You remember Violet, don't you? I brought her with me this evening."

Cullen smiled at Gadsden. His thoughts were still on KT, and he'd only heard about half of what Gadsden had said. "Probably just a coincidence," he said. He slapped his partner on the back. "I haven't wished you congratulations yet. No one deserves this award more." He grinned at the man who'd been a second father to him.

"Thanks." Gadsden smiled, but when Cullen turned away to speak to an acquaintance, the smile faded. Worry etched his features as he looked up the stairs again. Coincidence? He doubted it.

Krystal found the powder room. It was larger than her entire apartment, with a spacious ante-room whose walls were covered in beige linen scrolled in gold. She walked through to the wash-room, used the facilities, then went about the job of repairing the makeup Cullen had removed. She glared at her image, silently castigating herself for going overboard for Cullen Dempsey. "Use some restraint, for heaven's sake," she muttered at the mirror.

"You always did talk to yourself."

As the image of another woman appeared next to hers, Krystal gasped in shock. It had been a possibility that they would meet, but somehow she'd been sure it wouldn't happen.

"Violet," she breathed.

Four

The woman, who was only fifteen years older than she, who'd been Krystal's mother and mentor for three years, nodded. "Yes. It's a shock for me, too, Krystal. When you walked past me, I thought I was seeing things. I never expected to see you here. Somehow I thought you'd left California."

"I did . . . I have. Just visiting." Never had Krystal felt so stunned. She was quite sure if she moved, she'd fall. She was bleeding from a thousand cuts as her old life swirled around her, jabbing at her. Had she been a fool to think she could hide from it? "I ran," she blurted out. "You stayed and faced the music."

Violet Wynter shrugged. "Actually, there wasn't that much to face. I had a hearing and was cleared of the charges of fraud. Your father would've had to face that, too, if he'd lived." She smiled bleakly. "I couldn't find you."

Krystal shook her head slowly. "After my father

killed himself, I ran . . . and ran . . . and ran. Hitchhiked, took a bus, finally landed in Seattle."

Violet's eyes widened. "You went north. For some reason I thought you'd headed east. I made inquiries."

Krystal nodded, regret swamping her. "I'm sorry."

Violet put out her hand, then drew it back. "We weren't the culprits, Krystal." She smiled again, more happily. "You haven't changed. Maybe a little thinner, your eyes a little bigger." She added quietly, "It seems like another lifetime."

"It was." Krystal felt tears welling inside her.

For a moment the two women struggled with almost overwhelming emotions. Then it was tamped down and jammed out of the way.

"We can't stay in here forever," Violet said.

Krystal nodded. She had more to say, though. Taking a deep breath, she looked down at her hands. "I was so damned scared. But I never meant to leave you holding the bag."

Violet reached out again and this time touched Krystal's arm. "I never meant to compromise you in such a way. At first I closed my eyes to what your father was doing. Then . . . it was like being on a roller coaster. I couldn't get off. But once the damage was done and it was out in the open, I knew of no way to repair it except by facing down our accusers." She hesitated, studying the silk brocade that covered the settee on which they were sitting. "There are still some people who make remarks, who say I promoted fraud through prostitution, but I can handle them." She smiled. "I have a company now, that hires out temporary office help. It's called Wynterbreak and it's doing fine. And no one could fault it." She paused. "There's no way to tell you how sorry I am. But I am. I hope someday you'll believe me."

Krystal shook her head vigorously. "Don't, Vi. I'm the one who should be sorry. I ran. You stayed." She grasped the older woman's hand in both of hers. "I should've faced the music with you."

Violet squeezed her hand. "You loved your father. You didn't believe me when I told you that he could be in real trouble." She sighed. "Yes, you should've stayed, but you were crushed, first by his guilt, then by his death. You were in a dark hole, and I didn't know how to help you. You suffered so when it all came apart that way. I never wanted that."

Krystal nodded. "I know." She tried to smile. "I know now that Daddy led you into that life. He always wanted more—to succeed, to make a great deal of money." She shook her head again as chagrin, sadness, regret welled up in her. "He gravitated to the people who talked about 'easy' money and 'easy' ways to get it. Laundering money. How could he not know such schemes would involve him with criminals? Arranging parties that included questionable guests. Allowing illegal gambling at those parties. It was awful. He thought he'd be important, rich, respected."

"And he was destined not to have any of it," Violet said softly. "It hurt for a long time that he killed himself, but I've come to realize that it'd been bound to happen. He lived in a fantasy world. Reality beat him down to the ground."

The sound Krystal made was between a laugh and a sob. "He always thought he would find the Golden Fleece . . ."

"Just around the next corner." Violet nodded. "He was a dreamer who hated reality, and he got in over his head. But I still loved him."

"And for that, you let him draw you into a scheme where you would give parties for his clients." Krystal sighed. "I've only come around to this way of thinking recently. It was so much easier to blame you than my father." She stared at Violet. "I honestly don't think he thought it would go that far, or that—that group would involve itself."

"Len should've known you can't play games with the mob and not get hurt. But he was a dreamer, a foolish one. He should never have taken you from Pennsylvania."

Krystal tried to smile. "I was glad he did. I had no other relatives there. And though the neighbors were kind, I didn't want to marry any of their sons, which I would've had to do if I'd stayed."

Violet smiled faintly. "You were a lonely, big-eyed girl."

"Gawky and awkward."

"Sweet and hopeful," Violet countered. "You'd had a tough time after losing your mother."

"And you had one after losing my father."

Violet nodded. "It could've been worse." She grimaced. "If it hadn't been for a few friends vouching for me, I might have slipped through the cracks and been jailed." She exhaled heavily. "But let's not talk about that. Tell me what brings you to San Francisco and my friend's party."

"Your friend? Gadsden?"

Violet noted her reaction and bit her lip. "Yes.

He's one of the few who believed in me. He got a lawyer for me, and we won."

"I came with his partner." Krystal slumped helplessly against the back of the settee.

"Cullen Dempsey?" Violet's mouth opened in astonishment. "How?"

"I met him scrubbing floors. That's my business, cleaning offices at night. I started a business"—she grinned—"and it's taking off."

Violet tried to stop her happy laughter, but it couldn't be contained. "I love it. I absolutely love it. And your father worried that you wouldn't have the initiative to last in the world." She grabbed Krystal's hand. "Oh, my sweet girl, I'm so proud of you."

"Thank you," Krystal said absently, her thoughts back on Gadsden. "Do you know Cullen too?"

"I do. Krystal, darling, he's a wonderful person. He was also a help to me." Violet looked thoughtful. "I guess you were gone before I met Cullen. I like him. He's a fine man." She squeezed Krystal's hand, her gaze skating over her wristwatch at the same time. "Heavens. We've been here for ages. If we don't leave soon, those two men will send in a search party."

"Oh, no. You're right." Krystal leaped to her feet and wheeled toward the door.

"Remember, stroll," Violet said softly, as she'd often instructed the young Krystal.

Krystal looked over her shoulder. "I will." She reached back and touched her stepmother's arm. "Coming with me?"

Violet rose to her feet. "I had the feeling you might feel more comfortable on your own."

Krystal turned fully to face Violet. "No," she said firmly. "It would be just fine to have you at my side."

She took her stepmother's hand again. "I hope you'll forgive me one day for running out like that. I was so scared, so frightened of what could happen. Jail, disgrace, humiliation in the papers." She smiled ruefully. "Now, as I look back on it, I think I could've beaten them too."

Violet nodded. "I agree. And there's nothing to forgive, Krystal. I blame myself for letting Len influence me to do those foolish things. I knew better, understood the web tightening around us. I should've stopped him." She shook her head pensively, then glanced at Krystal. "But that's past. And now is now. Let's go, kid."

Krystal inhaled shakily, recalling how many times Violet had said that to her. She deeply regretted the two years of silence between her and her stepmother, but she wasn't entirely sorry she'd gone to Seattle. She'd developed a business that provided for her financially and was challenging. She had to compete for clients with other companies of the same caliber, and she was succeeding.

She wished with all her heart that she hadn't cannoned out of San Francisco as though the hounds of hell were at her heels, but she couldn't regret the growth she'd undergone in Seattle—or her meeting Cullen. Cullen! "I think we'd better hurry."

They left the ladies' room hand in hand, and for Krystal it felt strange but very good to walk at Violet's side again. Groups were clustered along the wide, carpeted corridor. Some people spoke to

Violet. She nodded to them, but didn't pause to speak.

"You still know everyone," Krystal murmured.

Violet smiled.

They reached the top of the stairs, and neither woman saw the men until they'd almost bumped into them.

"Well, what have we here?" Gadsden said heartily, his gaze darting between Violet and Krystal in uneasy awareness.

"Did you think I'd gotten lost, Gad?" Violet saw his consternation and patted his hand, then turned to the younger man. "How are you, Cullen? I haven't seen you in a while."

"Ah, no, Vi. That's true. How are you?" Cullen said haltingly, his gaze running over Krystal, then fixing on the women's clasped hands.

"Fine," Violet said. "So is Wynterbreak. I suppose Gad told you about that."

"Huh? Uh, maybe he did." Cullen's puzzled gaze settled on Krystal's face. "I didn't know you were acquainted with Violet." He'd had the same shivering sense of danger when facing the great white, the same tension that filled him now as he studied the woman who, in so short a time, had come to mean so much to him.

Krystal drew in a deep breath. "I told you I used to live in San Francisco. Violet is my stepmother."

"Your what?"

"Krystal is my stepdaughter." Violet glanced at the young woman standing next to her and smiled gently. "And one of my dearest friends."

"I see," Cullen said, his mouth dry, his brain on

hold. He didn't see, nor did he understand, but somehow he felt threatened.

When they were jostled by another guest and someone said hello, Gadsden and Violet turned away. Krystal and Cullen continued to stare at each other. When another person bumped into Cullen, he took Krystal's arm and moved her to one side, away from the flow of traffic up and down the staircase.

"I guess we didn't talk about a lot of things," Krystal said nervously, certain that Cullen would find out a great deal about her this evening. Information about her would snowball right at him, most of it damning. She lifted her chin. She'd run once. Not again. She didn't look away from Cullen, but one man's loud voice intruded as he stopped to speak to Violet and Gadsden.

"Violet, you look great. Our company used your temporaries, and we were very pleased, by the way. Damn, as I live and breathe, is that Krystal over there? It is. Krystal! Krystal, hello."

The man sidled around Violet to stand next to Krystal. She stared blankly at him, not recognizing him at all.

"How are you?" he asked. "I'll be wanting to dance with you when the music starts. For old times' sake. Why don't you come over here and give me a big hug, honey. Hey, Steve, look who I found."

Cullen's face seemed to freeze right in front of her. He glanced narrowly at the man, then back at her. "Krystal. I've heard that name. You were in demand," he said flatly, his eyes opaque, his meaning clear.

"So I was." She felt like crying, like shouting at

him to listen to her and not make snap judgments. She said nothing, though. Several men had joined their little group, driving a wider wedge between her and Cullen, literally and figuratively. Rooted to the spot, she tried to smile at the sea of faces, tried to respond to everyone.

"Hello. Yes, I remember you. Just fine. And you?" Words tumbled out of her. The man who'd first recognized her attempted to snatch her into a friendly bear hug. She backed up.

"Dammit," Cullen muttered, "get out of the way. You'll push her down the stairs."

Cullen's snarl and threatening manner were new facets of him, and they further unnerved Krystal. She stepped back involuntarily and felt her heel sink into air. "Ohh!"

"Damn!" Cullen snatched her back, pulling her against his chest and keeping her there with a hard arm around her shoulders.

"Thank you," she said into his tuxedo front. "I'm fine now." Too shaken to look up at him, she tried, to no avail, to free herself. In her presence Cullen had always been sweetness and laughter, gentle persuasion and teasing. Now he was thunder and barely leashed lightning.

She tried again to free herself. No go. He might as well have manacled her to him. There'd been a noticeable lessening in frivolity in their little corner.

"I think it must be time for us to take our seats," she heard Gadsden say. "Shall we go, Violet? Cullen, that was quick thinking. Krystal might've fallen down the stairs in the rush of well-wishers. Oh . . .

you two are at our table," he added weakly. "The head table."

"Great," Cullen said between his teeth. "That's all we needed." He was in a flat spin. His world was unraveling. Who the hell *was* KT? They'd called her Krystal. He'd heard of a woman with that name, well known in some circles, but she'd been . . . Hell!

"Well, if you think I'm any happier," Krystal began, ire building in her at his temper, "feel free to find another seat, and another dining companion. I'll find another table—"

"Let's go, Krystal," he said, interrupting her. "We're at the head table." He took her arm, just above the elbow, and propelled her down the stairs.

The temptation to struggle and send them both crashing down the stairs was a stupid reaction, and almost overwhelming. She settled for grabbing the banister and tugging him to a halt.

His head swung her way, like a bull on the charge.

"Do not," she said fiercely, "troll me along behind you as if I were a carp on a line."

"Well, my sweet," he said silkily, "you do have fangs and claws, don't you?"

"And I tear and bite, too, Dempsey." She continued down the stairs, then faced him. "And take that damned martyred expression off your face. I have no intention of staying in your company one second longer than necessary."

"Martyred?" Hearing his raised voice, people glanced inquiringly at him. He ignored them, glowering at the tall woman who faced him, chin up and looking as though she were boiling for a fight. Where had the reticent KT Wynter of Seattle gone? "I think you owe me an explanation. It would seem you're the former, but not forgotten, toast of San Francisco, who's misrepresented herself as—"

"I never misrepresented myself, to you or anyone else, nor do I owe you any explanation of my present, past, or future life. And if being in my company makes you uncomfortable, Mr. Dempsey, let me assure you that I can find an alternative way home." Krystal kept her voice low, anger having her in such a grip, she could barely keep from smacking him. She noticed that some people were still staring at them, but she was too furious to back off.

Cullen ground his teeth. "All this time you're Miss Milquetoast, saying only a few words, smiling sweetly, the perfect picture of a shy, retiring lady—"

"I am a lady, and shy only with some," she shot back.

"And, it would seem, friendly with others—"

"That does it." She punched him in the side, then whirled away from him, striding toward the exit.

He caught up with her at the elevator, putting his arms around her when she pushed against him. He saw the sheen of tears in her eyes, though she stared at him balefully. "Wait, KT . . . Krystal. I was out of line. I'm sorry about that last remark. It was uncalled for—"

"Damn straight," she said tautly.

"Come back with me to The Ballroom. We need to talk about this."

She shook her head. "No we don't. And I won't. I

meant what I said. I owe you no explanation, and you won't get one. So let me go. I'll get back to Seattle."

He shook his head. "Have it your way. But I brought you, and I'll fly you back." He glanced over his shoulder. "Right now, though, I think you should consider Gadsden and Violet and stay for the dinner."

He couldn't know that he'd struck the right chord with her. She'd run two years ago, and what had it done for her, other than make her reclusive and unsociable? No more! she decided. This evening had solidified her shaky decision to begin living a normal life again. She'd done nothing wrong. She'd been accused by some as being other than what she was, and she should have fought back. Running away had hurt her, and Violet. "All right," she said. "I'll stay for the dinner, then I'll—"

"I'll fly you home," he finished implacably.

Turning away from him, mouth compressed in a tight line, she walked into the dining room.

When she saw the look of relief on Violet's face, she could only be glad she'd chosen to stay. And since she was seated next to the older woman, she could carry on a conversation with her and ignore Cullen.

During the soup course, she asked Cullen to pass the black pepper. When salad was served, he asked her for the grated cheese. During the entree, they each passed the rolls once and said thank you. When the chocolate mousse came, they dutifully handed each other the cream. While the liqueurs were passed, they kept their attention fixed on the various speakers honoring Gadsden, although neither heard a word of what was said. Finally Gadsden rose to give his thanks, and it was over.

Krystal shot to her feet.

Gadsden touched her arm. "I hope you're going to let me lead you out to the dance floor, my dear. We haven't had much chance to talk."

She hesitated, but the pleading look in his eyes had her smiling and nodding. "Thank you. I'd like that."

He exhaled, looking pleased. "Good."

The twosome started toward the dance floor, stopping now and then to speak to people. The minute the quintet began to play, Gadsden took Krystal's arm and led her onto the floor.

Cullen ignored the people around him and stared at the dancing couple.

"You're frowning," Violet said.

He glanced at her. "Sorry. Tell me how you're doing, Violet."

"That false smile and interest don't fool me, Cullen Dempsey. You want to ask me about Krystal." She stared up at him. "She's not had it easy, but I've yet to hear her complain."

"She's just an all-American girl," he said.

"Don't be cute, Cullen. It's not for me to explain Krystal to you. If she wants you to know, she'll tell you. But I will say this: What happened to her here in San Francisco was very painful. And it was none of her doing."

Cullen saw the hurt and anger in Violet's face, the way her hands flexed in agitation, but he was too caught up in his own turmoil to give it his full attention. "Sorry. I wasn't aiming any of this at you."

"And don't aim your bad feelings at her, either," Violet said. "She's had enough of men betraying her and castigating her."

He froze, his gaze sharpening on Violet as a knot slowly tightened inside him. He didn't want to know, but he had to ask. "What do you mean?"

Violet's lips tightened. "Nothing." She turned away to speak to someone passing.

"Violet," Cullen said quietly.

She turned back to him, shaking her head. "I've said too much already. Talk to Krystal."

Cullen all but gasped with pain as his imagination conjured pictures in vivid color of Krystal and other men. Wasn't that what her life had been? He was fuzzy on details, but . . . How many men had been in her life? Did she still have feelings for any of them? Had any of them visited her in Seattle? Had there been a special one? His blood burned like acid. Did it matter? he asked himself. Yes, dammit, it did. He wanted to be the important man in her life, the only one. He wanted to ask her how she felt about them being together all the time. No, he couldn't let her past matter, not if he wanted to stay sane.

His gaze strayed to the dance floor again, and he saw her at once. Gadsden was no longer her partner. The man who'd first spoken to her when they'd been on the second floor was now laughing down at her, holding her in his arms. As Cullen watched, his hands clenching into fists, another man approached and cut in, taking a smiling Krystal in his arms.

"May I get you a drink, sir?"

Cullen stared blankly at the waiter who'd appeared at his side, then snapped, "Yes. Old Bushmill's. Make it a double." The waiter nodded and melted away.

Violet, who'd been chatting with some other guests, heard him order and moved back to his side. "I won't let her fly with you, if you're going to drink heavily," she said. "I've found her again. I won't lose her because you're caught in some macho web of your own making."

His smile twisted, Cullen looked down at the diminutive woman with the frosted hair. "You don't pull your punches, do you, Violet? Don't worry. I'll be cold sober by the time we leave. It's been a damn sobering night."

"It hasn't been a picnic for her, either."

"A tough evening all around," he said bitingly, and took his drink from the waiter.

"Yes, it has been. And remember that." Violet smiled with relief as she saw Gadsden approaching them.

"Are you all right, my dear?" he asked, sliding his arm around her waist. He glanced questioningly at Cullen.

"I wouldn't worry about her," Cullen said. "She's been standing there slicing and dicing me while she carries on an ultracivilized conversation with everyone else."

Gadsden eyed the drink in Cullen's hand, then frowned when the younger man tossed back half of it. "Are you flying back this evening?"

"I am." He set the glass down on a nearby table so forcefully, he almost shattered the heavy crystal.

"I can see I'd better do something other than drink as long as you two are going to ogle me like a couple of Carry Nations." He strolled away from them without another word, heading toward the dance floor.

"What do you think, my dear?" Gadsden asked Violet.

"I think four people sustained shocks tonight," she murmured, shaking her head. "I'm still reeling, but Cullen got the worst hit."

Gadsden nodded. "Coincidences like this rarely happen. And I wish it could've happened under more private circumstances."

"Coincidence? Is that how you see this? I think not. I think the angels who've always guarded Krystal have taken a hand again." Violet smiled. "Admittedly, they've proven to have somewhat barbed senses of humor, but I think she's on a happier road . . . and I think Cullen's part of it. Don't laugh at me. I know how it looks now, but I believe it."

"I'm not laughing," Gadsden said. "Maybe those same angels will save Cullen."

Violet smiled fondly at him. "You love him, don't you?"

"Yes. He's all any man would want in a son. And his life hasn't exactly been a bed of roses."

"You told me his mother walked out on his father, and the father began drinking."

"Cullen's father drank himself to death," Gadsden said succinctly.

They clasped hands, silently giving each other strength, and their glances strayed to the dance floor.

Krystal didn't see him coming. Cullen could tell that. She was relaxed, laughing at something her partner had said as they swayed to the Latin beat.

He tapped the other man on the shoulder, and his scowl was enough to make the man release Krystal and walk away.

Krystal looked pointedly past Cullen's ear. "Is it time to go?" she asked.

"Soon." He took her in his arms, and immediately forgot everyone else in the room. She was like a rose—fragile, colorful, beautiful—and her body curved into his so naturally, even when she was trying to hold herself stiff. But she had thorns too. He'd felt those tonight. "You're a good dancer," he said.

"Thank you." Her voice was muffled because she was looking away from him.

He couldn't think of another thing to say to her. Hell, he just wanted to dance with her, hold her. But there was a wall between them a mile high and half again as deep.

"I assumed when you cut in," Krystal said, "that you'd like to go soon." What else would be his reason for coming out to dance with her? But that was fine, she told herself. She only wanted to get away from him too. It galled her to think of all the things he'd probably heard about her that evening. He would've heard plenty, and it wouldn't end there. Now that the gate was open, there'd be a deluge of information whenever he mentioned her name to certain people in this area. She couldn't smother the gossip, but it nauseated her to think of him believing any of it—and a great deal had a plausible ring to it. She'd be damned, though, if she'd explain.

Tears rained down on her soul as she thought how it might have been. The two of them dancing to the pulsing ballad. Cullen making her laugh, saying sweet things that she longed to hear. Now he never would. There was too wide a chasm between them. But she'd survived before. She'd survive this.

"Whenever you're ready to leave," Cullen said tautly. She was obviously eager to get rid of him. Now that she'd renewed acquaintance with her San Francisco friends, she didn't need him in her life. Damn her.

"I'm ready now." He couldn't wait to get rid of her, she thought. "In fact, if you like I could see if I could get a commercial—"

"Never mind. I'll take you."

As soon as the music was over, they turned as though on some hidden signal and strode across the ballroom, smiles pasted to their mouths.

"I'll call you soon," Krystal promised Violet, kissing her on the cheek. Despite the horrible time with Cullen, she'd renewed her relationship with her stepmother. She felt buoyed by that.

"If you don't call, I'll be up there," Violet said, waving the business card Krystal had given her. "I've missed you so much," she added quietly.

"And I, you." Krystal saw the tears glistening in Violet's eyes and hugged her again before turning away with Cullen.

Gadsden and Violet watched them go.

"They looked good together," Violet said sadly.

Gadsden squeezed her arm. "That's nothing to be sad about, is it?"

She shrugged. "I don't know. I have a feeling that nothing will come of that relationship now."

"Not twenty minutes ago you told me that angels had arranged the evening for Krystal."

"They might've been black angels."

"Because so many people here knew Krystal?"

"That, and the uncomfortable position Cullen's in now. I could tell by the way he looked at her when we came out of the powder room that he thought her pretty special." She bit her lip. "Then when he found out who she was and Waterston blustered in with his friends, he looked as though someone had punched him in the stomach."

"I hope you're wrong, Violet," Gadsden said. "He could use some love in his life."

"So could she."

The night sky over California was a swath of black velvet with glistening crystals all across its surface. As they flew north the sky misted over as though the world had begun to cry.

Krystal felt pretty teary herself. When she'd first met Cullen, she'd expected nothing to last between them. After a while, she'd been lulled into believing she might be able to keep him. She'd fallen to earth hard that night, and she'd carry the bruises for the rest of her life.

Cullen wanted to speak to Krystal, but he didn't know what to say. Should he ask her why she hadn't told him? Why she'd been deceitful? He wanted to say he understood, but he didn't. He was so damned mad, his mouth was full of vinegar and curses.

When Cullen didn't speak, Krystal told herself she should say something. Her tongue seemed glued to the roof of her mouth, though. Why didn't he talk to her? Perhaps he was still numb with shock. Or maybe he was filled with an acidic fury he was trying desperately to control.

She was grateful she'd seen Violet again, had talked with her, dissolving all of her ghosts and goblins. If only she hadn't had to lose Cullen. Her heart and soul were gone now. She'd been stupid two long years ago in San Francisco and now had to pay for it by losing him. Damn, damn stupidity. Tears filled her eyes. Sobs clogged her throat and tore at her head, starting a throbbing that soon became a full-blown headache.

Cullen circled the airfield, then landed smoothly, in spite of the pain whirling through him like a tornado. He was losing her. Dammit! He was losing her.

He drove her home, the soft roar of the Porsche's engine the only sound in the car. He stopped in front of her building.

"Good night, Krystal."

"Good night, Cullen."

Parting wasn't sweet sorrow. It was jagged, rasping anguish.

Five

The weeks after the dinner-dance honoring Gadsden were hollowed-out seconds and minutes that dripped into hours and days.

Wet snow fell nearly every day through February, clinging to clothing and eyelashes, heavy and burdensome. Walking was a sloshing motion that splashed the gray slush upward onto boots and trousers. Standing curbside became a dangerous occupation, and people hung back cautiously until the light changed. The sky was so bulky and overweight with gray clouds, it was a miracle it didn't collapse in clumps on the streets.

For Krystal, life was living in a drum. She felt the thrumming all around her, shaking through her blood, thumping from her head to her feet. Words echoed and bounced off her. Some penetrated, but not many. Work was her salvation, and she poured herself into it from wake time to sleep time. With anything else her attention span was nil. She ran out of milk, the cheese got moldy, the bread turned drier than the Sahara. She finally bought milk, canned soup, three boxes of unsalted saltines, and a bag of oranges, and shoved everything, including the saltines, into the refrigerator. Then it was back to the grind.

The harder she worked, the better she slept, and then she didn't dream. So each day she went at it a little more grimly, munching saltines and sipping milk. Coffee and tea made her gag. Whenever she passed a restaurant on the street, she held her breath. Most food smells made her ill, and she had no wish to empty her innards on the sidewalk. She didn't notice as the weight began to drop. Her coveralls were baggy; her skirts slid around her waist.

Work was her solace and, miracle of miracles, it was taking off. She spent her days doggedly going through the phone book, trying to drum up business. What had started as a sense-numbing, monotonous method of forgetting began paying off in contracts.

New orders rolled in, and she relished the extra paperwork. Since she was office manager, clerk, and secretary, she had mountains of it. Despite that, she filled in whenever anyone was unable to report for work—though not in Cullen's building. That she didn't even try to face.

His name was enough to make her tremble. Not all her efforts could eradicate him from her mind. To salt the wound, two weeks after the San Francisco trip there was a write-up on him and his company in the local paper. And there was a picture of him. Despite herself, she carefully cut

out the article and picture and put them in the
drawer of her bedside table.

Every time the phone rang she jumped. Every
time the bell above the door of her new shop
jangled, signaling someone entering or exiting,
she'd drop whatever she held in her hand. She was
thankful her apartment was just upstairs. She
often made trips up there for aspirin.

Early one afternoon she had some free time and
decided to paint the cornice board that masked
the wall lights in the shop. She was on the top step
of the ladder, painting meticulously, since below
the cornice was a pickled maple paneling that
she'd had cleaned by specialists so that it gleamed
richly.

When the bell over the door jangled, she turned,
brush in hand, then gaped. Cullen! For a moment
she was sure she'd conjured him up. No. He was
there, as big as life, wearing a business suit of the
best worsted and a silk tie. She fought the quivers
that went through her as she carefully turned back
around. Her hand shaking, she tried to put the
brush back in the paint tray. Her trembling shook
the ladder, though, and it rocked precariously. She
tried to grab the cornice to steady herself, but her
hand slipped on the wet paint. The paint tray
shifted. She grabbed for that, accidentally knock-
ing it more askew. In slow motion, everything took
on a life of its own.

"Dammit!" Cullen exclaimed. "Are you trying to
kill yourself?" He dove forward and clutched the
teetering ladder.

Krystal finally got purchase on the cornice and

reached for the slipping tray. But her hand again slipped on the paint-slicked cornice, further unbalancing her. She struggled to brace herself, making the ladder tip crazily, even as Cullen was reaching up for her.

"Ohhhh!" she cried as the tray lost the battle with gravity.

"Damn!" Cullen swore as paint rained down over his suit, its rich black-blue hue spattered with #7/62, Old World Ecru, eighteen seventy-nine a gallon. "Dammit! Krystal!" He blindly put a hand up to steady her, his fingers curling around her buttocks, his eyes shut against a freshet of paint in his face.

She peeked down at him as the world settled back in place. "Oh. Your suit has paint on it," she said lamely.

"Thank you for that shrewd observation," he said, his free hand swiping ineffectually at the paint.

"Oh." She sighed.

"If you say 'Oh' one more time . . ." He helped her down the ladder and stared at her, hands on his hips.

"Of course, I'll pay for the cleaning," she mumbled, unable to meet his gaze.

"Damn straight. Not that I think it will help."

"Don't glare at me. It wasn't my fault you made the ladder wobble."

"Me? I made the ladder wobble?"

"And don't shout." She glared at him, chin up and her heart thudding in her chest. She'd seen him so much in her dreams, she had a hard time believing he was really there. She glanced at his suit again and winced. "Why don't you go in the back room? I have some clean coveralls hanging on hooks back there. Take off your suit, and I'll run it over to the cleaner's across the street. Mr. Dangeli is very good and very careful. If anyone can—" But she was talking to air. Cullen had already pushed through the curtain and was crashing around in the back room. "Temper tantrum," she said huffily to herself. "Of all things!" He looked the same, she mused. But was there a touch of gray in his hair? Maybe he was a few pounds thinner. He still looked wonderful. Too bad about his suit, though.

A hand came through the curtain, holding out his jacket and pants. "Here. Take them to the cleaner's. Ask him if I can have them in an hour. I have a luncheon appointment."

"Don't worry, Mr. Dangeli is a marvel. It's water-based paint, so we can be thankful for that."

"What a comfort."

She glared at the curtain. "Well, you needn't be so caustic. I didn't do it on purpose. You startled me."

"Do you do that to every customer?"

"You're not a customer."

"I might be."

"Hah!"

"Don't scoff. Gadsden and I decided we wanted another location nearer the waterfront. We've bought one of the old buildings down there and are having it renovated."

He'd only come to sign up her services as a cleaning lady! she thought. The gall of the man. "I see. Well, I'll give you a brochure with our prices when I return from the dry cleaner's."

"Thank you."

"You're welcome." She waited there for a moment longer, hoping he might say more. Then she castigated herself for being a fool. There was nothing between them any longer.

She put his suit in a clean bag, donned her old down jacket, and left, feeling miserable.

The trip to Dangeli's took mere minutes. When she returned Cullen was behind the counter talking to a man she had never seen before. She opened the door. The bell jangled.

. . . and with that," Cullen was saying, "you'll get the best night crew available. And at a lower price than most other cleaners charge."

The man said something she couldn't hear. Krystal stared, but she didn't move. She was too canny not to notice when a customer was teetering on a yes decision.

At last the two men shook hands, the customer signed a receipt, and Cullen ran the man's credit card through the machine.

Krystal stepped aside as the man left, smiling at him. Then the bell jangled and the door banged shut.

Silence.

"Will my suit be ready in an hour?" Cullen asked, swallowing a laugh. She'd gone to the cleaner's with a dab of paint on her nose and a soft spray of off-white on her eyebrows.

"What? Oh, no, but Mr. Dangeli thinks he can remove the paint. It'll take time, though."

"What? I have an appointment." He glanced at his watch and cursed. "In twenty-five minutes ."

"What were you doing with that man?"

"What man? Oh. The customer. He was interested in getting his offices cleaned. He's a manager for an insurance firm. Ten offices on one floor, six on another. He gave me a retainer." He shoved the billing slip at her, then looked around, his jaw clenching. "I've got to get back to my office and get my car."

Taking a deep breath, Krystal shook the bill in his face.

"How do you know I have the time or the staff to handle this? It was a little high-handed of you, wasn't it?"

He looked at her. "Better to send him on his way to another outfit? That's a great way to get business."

She bristled. "I don't need your help to get business. As it happens I—"

"I don't have time for a debate. I'm in a hurry. I walked over here from my office." He ignored her questioning look. He wasn't about to tell her that he'd needed the several-block hike to work up the courage to talk to her. He hadn't been able to stay away any longer, but he hadn't been sure of what his reception might be, either. The spilled paint had been an unexpected diversion, and it had helped and hindered. She hadn't thrown him out, but they hadn't discussed their relationship. Dammit! He was living his life walking a tightrope. It had to stop.

"I'll drive you," she said grudgingly. Who'd asked him to come to her place anyway, to walk those ten—or was it twelve—blocks? He had no business coming back into her life. She was getting better. She was able to go great stretches of time without thinking of him . . . sometimes as long as an hour. And she was dealing with her life. Why did he have to come by and make her spill paint?

"Well, don't stand there dreaming," he said. "We have to go." She looked damn cute with paint on her face, he thought, her hair spilling out from beneath a cotton paint cap that advertised Yardley's stirrers, guaranteed not to break when stirring the thickest paint.

"My van's out back," she said. "I just have to clean out my brush and top the can." She got enough money from her purse to cover the cleaning bill, then handed it and the receipt for his suit to him. Not looking at him, she put the CLOSED sign in the window and stalked past him to the back room, carrying the paintbrush and tray.

She was surprised when he began to work alongside her at the big washtub in the back, where the cleaning equipment was scrubbed each night. "Excuse me," she said when they were finished. "I'll just slip off my coveralls."

Before she could move, he took her arms. "Aren't you going to look at me?"

"I did." She glanced up and away.

"I've missed you."

"You said you were late," she said desperately, on the verge of tears and determined not to let him see how his words affected her.

"So I did." He released her and watched as she all but ran into a small cubicle and pulled the curtain. "Damn!" he muttered. He'd thought of her con-

stantly ever since they'd parted weeks ago. He'd
been on the verge of calling her more than a dozen
times. She obviously hadn't had any trouble forgetting him, though. When she reappeared clad in
tight jeans and a cotton sweater, slinging a shear-
ling coat over her shoulder, he stared at her. She
was sensuous, provocative, sexy as hell, yet she
looked like an innocent virgin at the same time.

"Let's go," Krystal said, anxiously noticing how
he stared at her. Was he recalling Gadsden's party
and the rush of men who'd come up to her? Had he
heard about her since then and dropped by to
assess her? Well, to hell with him. Her heart
squeezed and she cursed her body and mind for
giving themselves over to such a man. He had
sailed through the door of her life, wreaked havoc
on her, and thought he could get away with it. To
hell with him!

He indicated the coveralls he was wearing. "I'll
get these back to you."

"Fine."

They walked outside to the messy area behind
her building that was a stash for various pieces of
junk, now covered with snow. She'd cleared a big
enough space for her van, but the rest of the
cleanup would have to wait for spring.

Cullen studied the rust-pocked van, a dented,
vintage junker with two bent bumpers. The door
squeaked and sagged when he yanked it open, as
did Krystal's. His gaze ran over the torn upholstery
and the cluttered back.

"It runs well and gets good mileage," she said
stiffly.

"Good." Krystal certainly was a fighter, he

thought. The van had to be a bitch to shift. He could tell that, top-heavy as it was, with ladders and other paraphernalia perched on top, it would be hard to steer. It was too old to have power steering.

She ground the gears when she backed it up, and color ran up her neck.

"Have you heard from Violet?" he asked quickly, pretending not to notice.

She nodded as she backed around in the small clearing until she faced a narrow driveway between her building and the one next door. When she reached the street, she paused, sized up the traffic, found an opening, and gunned it, slamming the gear into second. Griiinnnndd. "Yes," she said, safely on the street. "She calls me a couple of times a week and on weekends. She's coming up to stay in the not-too-distant future."

"Good. She and Gadsden have become pretty close. I wouldn't be surprised if he tried to persuade her to marry him."

Krystal's head swung his way, and the van veered.

"Careful!" Cullen leaned over and grabbed the wheel, steering it back to its lane with difficulty. "This damned thing is a lumbering elephant, too much for you to handle."

"It works well for my company," she said loftily. "I hope you're not thinking that Violet isn't good enough for Gadsden. He's a very nice person, but Violet is wonderful and she—"

"I never thought she was anything but a good person, Krystal." He gazed at her profile, gritting his teeth as he noticed her stiffening her muscles in order to steer the large vehicle. "I think I know where I can get my hands on a sleeker van than this." He hated seeing her drive this rust monster. And he could tell by its sway and unwieldiness that it wouldn't serve her well in a driving crisis.

"This suits me fine," Krystal said hurriedly. She refused to be beholden to him. She already felt too caught up in his power. Besides, the van was all she could afford for the time being. She was making only a marginal profit on her business. She didn't dare sink money into another vehicle.

"All right," he said, obviously not pleased with her refusal.

She pulled up in front of his building and glanced over at him. "You'll have to hurry. You don't have much time."

"Thank heavens I have another suit in the office." He turned toward her as he unbuckled his seat belt. "I'd like to see you again, Krystal. We need to talk. Maybe we could have dinner."

"I don't think so." Have dinner with him and have him stare at her, recalling all the things people doubtlessly had said to him about her. No.

"All right," he said again, not even bothering to hide his scowl. "See you."

"Right."

He got out, and she barely waited for him to close the door before pulling out into traffic. She heard him yell at the same time that a driver leaned on his horn and shook his fist at her. She mouthed her regret to the driver, but didn't look back at Cullen. Shoving him from her mind was impossible, but she did try to concentrate more on her driving.

• • •

Gadsden walked into Cullen's office late that afternoon and found him staring out the window. "What's up?"

"I've decided to go back to sea. I think I could use some hands-on time with the fishing. We have some very lucrative contracts, and it wouldn't be a bad idea for me to keep tabs on the catches for a while."

"I see," Gadsden said slowly. "Any special reason you've decided this?"

Cullen threw the papers he was holding down on his desk. He threw them so hard, they scattered a few pens and pencils, and some slipped onto the floor. "Yes. I need to go."

Gadsden bent to pick up the pencils. "Have you seen Krystal?" he asked mildly.

"Yes, damn her to hell. She's too thin, and she works like she's getting paid overtime. You should see what she drives. A damn rusty Sherman tank that she can barely steer. What the hell is the matter with her?" He flung himself down in his swivel chair and banged his fist on the desk.

"Once," Gadsden said, settling himself in another chair, "when you were just beginning to go out on the boats with your father and me, you tied a line wrong. One of the trollers loosened, then pulled away . . ."

"You needn't retell the story," Cullen said tightly. "I was there. Nielsen was hurt because of me. It could've been very serious."

"And afterward you were the subject of biting ridicule from the crew. You could've been taken off the *Mary Bee* and put on the *Deirdre*, but you chose to stick it out. Why?"

Cullen frowned at his friend. "This is totally irrelevant to our discussion."

"I don't think so. Answer me."

He shrugged, annoyed, uncomfortable. "I'm no fool. You're trying to draw some sort of analogy between—"

"Answer," Gadsden said inexorably.

Cullen jumped to his feet, beginning to pace. "All right. I toughed it out because I knew I couldn't ever face those guys if I didn't handle it. So?"

Gadsden smiled. "That's what Krystal's doing. Toughing it out, alone, as she's done since leaving San Francisco."

"Now wait a minute, her situation is different. She isn't facing me, she's avoiding me."

Gadsden exhaled, looking disgusted. "You're blind, man. You, who used to be one of the most perceptive men I've ever known, don't see it. Didn't it occur to you that she might not be sure you didn't believe all that gossip about her?"

Cullen glared at him. "I didn't believe any of it! Krystal as a high-priced 'business companion,' as call girls are euphemistically known these days? No, I don't buy it."

"And you punched out Carter Begging when he made a snide reference to Krystal."

"You heard about that?"

"It made the news services, I think," Gadsden said dryly.

"No, it didn't. Begging had it coming." Cullen absently reached down and pulled on his suit coat. "Handle things here. I'll be out for a while."

"How long?"

"However long it takes. Just say I've gone fishin'."

Gadsden grinned as Cullen stalked out of the office, slamming the door behind him. Then he ambled over to Cullen's desk and dialed a number. "Violet? Gadsden. I think things are looking up, darlin'."

Dirty and spattered with paint, Krystal closed the office, yawning hugely. She needed some time off. Thank goodness she had a full complement of workers for the night. Clapping a hand over a yawn big enough to dislocate her jaw, she finished her filing and closed the drawer with a snap.

Soaking in her bathtub for eight hours might wash some of the weariness from her, she mused. Submerging herself for a year might cleanse from her spirit the lead weights of regret.

Upstairs in her apartment, she handled the last bit of business she had to do before she could relax. She checked the logbook, called each place where her workers were, and went down the list of tasks with each manager. "All right, call if there are any glitches," she told the last one, then hung up the phone, sighing with relief. She stripped off her clothes and dropped them into the small stack washer that had been fitted into a small closet off the kitchen.

It was supper time, but she was too worn out to eat. She poured herself a tall glass of milk and carried it into the bathroom.

Lowering herself into the tub, she drank her milk slowly, then set the empty glass on the floor.

Smiling, she closed her eyes and sank deeper into the fragrant water, blowing at the bubbles. Heaven. Paradise. A king's ransom of delight. She had no idea of time, only a joyous release of tension as her body swayed gently in the hot scented water. The music from her stereo out in the living room was like a rhythmic backdrop to her relaxation.

"You should lock your door when you're in the tub."

"Aaagh!" Krystal reared up, sloshing water over the sides of the tub, splashing it in her eyes, sliding and banging her elbow, as she fought for control of her mind and body. Cullen! She'd conjured him up by wanting him so much! Her blood pressure must be a 100 over 1000. She'd be dead in ten minutes or less.

"Shall I wash you?" he asked.

Startled, flabbergasted, she sank back into the water, then came back up sputtering and flailing, her eyes closed. "Who is it?" She knew damn well who it was, but she fought for time, arms crossed over her breasts. "Get out of here." Damn him, she thought, sneaking a peek at him. He was beautiful. Irritating. And that wonderful body . . . The pervert. How dare he seduce her with his looks? She'd have him arrested . . . after she kissed him six or seven thousand times. Oh, damn, she wanted him. "Leave."

"Calm down," Cullen said soothingly. "You know who it is. You looked right at me." He stared at her creamy-pink body, what he could see around mountains of bubble bath and wisps of steam, and thought he'd have his first heart attack. She was incredibly beautiful, strong and shapely. The sight of her sent his heart banging hard against his rib cage. He'd written her name on memos to the Bridgeton Fish Mongers in Newfoundland. He'd scrawled her initials on a fax to Juneau, Alaska. Just the day before he'd called Gadsden "Krystal." His wise partner had let it pass. She had to talk to him; she was wrecking his life. Dammit, he needed her.

"Cullen Dempsey!" she exclaimed. "How dare you walk into my home like this. Trespasser. Voyeur. Burglar—"

"Will you put a sock in it? They can hear you on the docks. Let me explain. I had no intention of entering your apartment. But you left the door unlocked. Stupid."

"I didn't, and don't call me stupid," she said, trying to swipe the soap from her eyes.

"You did." He wet a face cloth with warm water and pressed it to her face. "Here. Don't rub, just wipe gently."

"Don't tell me what to do," she said acidly, dabbing at her soap-stung eyes. "Get out of here."

"I'll get you out of there first. In the mood you're in, you could take a flying leap in that claw-footed monster and crack your head. Where the hell did you get this damn thing?"

"It came with the place, and I'll have you know that claw feet on tubs are all the rage." She winced when she tried to open her eyes. "Get out of here," she said again, squinting through one eye.

"No. You could fall."

"Hand me a towel then." How was she going to get out of the tub with him there? "You wait for me in the other room. I'll only be a minute." When he shook his head, she cuffed water at him. He was so damned sexy in his pleated trousers, she thought. And his fine cotton shirt showed off his biceps. Exhibitionist. He had the greatest pecs . . . and thighs . . . and his hair was so luxuriant . . .

"Get out of here." She glared, splashing more water toward him.

"Damn. At least it isn't paint this time," he muttered, swiping at the bubbles on his trousers. "We have to talk, Krystal."

"Fine. Go out in the other ro—"

"No." He wanted to hold her, make love to her, have her love him.

Before she could react in any way, he reached down and lifted her straight up and out of the tub, standing her on the soft bath mat. While she was still sputtering and ineffectually pushing at him, he picked up the plastic bottle of moisturizer sitting on the sink and poured some onto his hands. "Keeps away the winter itch if you put it on wet skin," he said as he began massaging her with it. His hands tingled from touching her exciting body. He loved it. "Of course, spring's almost here. The snow's gone." He was shaking with desire. He could have made love to her right there on the bathroom floor.

"Stop," she said weakly.

"I can't," he whispered. Touching her was all the wonder and beauty he could ever want, now and a thousand years into the future.

Krystal tried again. "You wanted to talk." She was melting right into the tile floor. She wanted him to make love to her, right that very minute.

"I still do," he said huskily. She was so beautiful, so incredibly sexy, passionate, wonderful.

"Then talk." Her body was turning to liquid. "I don't do this," she added insanely. "Entertain when I'm taking a bath." She was talking non-sense! Her brain was mush.

"I don't either. As a matter of fact, I've never dried off a woman after a bath. I like it."

"You weren't invited to do this."

"I'm spontaneous." He leaned down and kissed her lips.

"That's not part of the deal."

"I've missed you." He'd been in pieces without her.

"Have you?" She'd been grief-stricken without him, unable to sleep.

"Yes." He never wanted to be parted from her again.

"You're beautiful," he went on. Never in all his years, since his first encounter with females at fifteen, had he ever felt so totally off balance. Krystal had done it to him, and he had the sensation of floating aimlessly even as he clasped her tightly to him. He frowned down at her.

Confused by the mixture of ardor and anger in his eyes, Krystal tried to push back from him. She fought the heat invading her limbs, the need to give herself to him, even as she struggled to understand the message in his mesmerizing eyes. The sudden down-twisting of his mouth gave her pause. "What are you thinking?"

"Many confluent rivers of thought about you, lady." At her sudden stiffening, he smiled, one finger touching her mouth. "Easy. Relax. I was thinking how independent, hardworking, and persistent you are. A tough and yet most ladylike woman, Krystal." His mouth traced her chin and jawline up to her ear. He nibbled there. "We had a great thing going."

"Ridiculous," she said breathlessly. "We hardly knew each other." But she had known him. He'd changed her life, bringing the sunshine back into it. He'd made her face what she'd put on the back porch of her mind, and in doing that had forced her to take a good hard look at herself. Her fingers dug into his shoulders, as though the tactile exploration would mark him more deeply in her memory. She was still certain he'd go eventually, but he'd live in her mind for years to come.

"We did 'know' each other in a very committed way," he said. "We just skipped a few steps in the normal routine."

"It was a roller-coaster ride," she said, trying to smile.

"It was solid, healthy, and bright as the sun," he said urgently, a little embarrassed at his own intensity. Abruptly, he tightened his hold, pressing his mouth into her hair.

Taken aback by his sudden tension, she tried to laugh. "Sounds a little like an environmental plan," she said.

He laughed, too, his tongue touching the creamy skin of her neck. "Don't deny we were traveling a road side by side, Krystal."

"A bumpy road, full of ruts and curves."

"Most relationships find the same thing," he said huskily.

"And then things happen." Loneliness, emptiness . . . and yearning.

"To everyone, not just us. We've been lucky, in a way." He leaned back from her. "We found out about each other quickly, publicly, but we haven't foundered. Everyone has to take some shots."

"Yes, they do. Many times, all through their lives."

He shrugged. "So? We'll take it one at a time."

Was he talking about a future? she wondered. Hope rushed through her.

His crooked smile was almost her undoing, but memory thrust between them. "And if it's too much?" she asked. "Too many disruptions, distractions, disillusionment? Then what?"

"That's why people protect precious moments, keep them alive in their minds." He studied her, her flushed skin, the wary wonder growing in her eyes. "No one person gets it all. There's enough heartbreak to spread around to each and every person on the planet, lady."

"And your solution?"

"There's a bitter irony in much of life. But"—he caressed her cheek with his lips—"if we harvest the good things, deal with the bad and then discard them, we'll stay on the high road. And that's all anybody gets, darlin'."

"So we have to build a treasure chest, do we?"

"That's the idea." He held himself still, not daring to move, wondering if he could trust the loving glint in her eyes.

"I can see that," she said. And she did want to build that treasure chest with Cullen. He had been a beacon in her life, his light illuminating her dark soul. Feeling giddy, she let her hands do what they'd been itching to do—rise to his head and thread and rethread through the thick strands of hair.

"I want to make love to you so badly," he said hoarsely, "I'm weak in the knees. But I need to talk about us more." He swallowed heavily, lowering his forehead to hers.

"I'm not sure I'll let you make love to me." What a bold-faced lie! She wanted nothing more than to hold him, to have him inside her. "We should know where we're going," she added. What bunk! All she wanted was to stay in his arms.

"Fine." Cullen tried to smile over his keen disappointment. "No lovemaking for now. It was just a suggestion." It was the request of his life. He really wanted to ask her to marry him, but somehow he didn't think she'd go for that at the moment.

She nodded. "But we should talk. If you get out of here, I'll dress."

He didn't move. His feet were glued to the floor. "Krystal?" He stared down at the wonderful, exciting vee of her breasts where they rose, creamy-pink, above the slipping towel.

"Yes."

"If all goes well with us, will you do me a favor?"

"Depends." Anything in the world, she thought, as long as he didn't leave her.

"I'd like to take a bath with you in the claw-footed monster," he said, then squeezed his eyes shut as though in pain. "That's after we settle everything, of course," he added through gritted teeth.

"What's the matter?" She rubbed his cheek tenderly.

"I'm trying not to picture you and me in that damned tub, but I'm having a tough time." Her body would glow with health, and shiny bubbles would cling to her nipples—"Damn!"

"Imagination can be tough." Images flashed through her own mind and she felt weak again. "Intolerable," she said hoarsely.

"Tell me about it." He clutched her to him. "We'd better eat, or go play chess, or ice-skate."

"You're babbling," she murmured.

"Can't help it." Not with desire raging through him like an inferno.

She looked up at him. "There's a great deal at stake here," she said solemnly.

"My sanity, for one thing." He kissed her. "You've got a fight on your hands, Wynter, because I want this."

"You're in for a battle yourself, Dempsey, because I want it, too, but under certain conditions."

"Are we talking about a pre-live-in agreement?"

Startled, she leaned back from him. She hadn't meant that at all, but she could see why he would. He was a tough businessman who would read the fine print of any contract. "Ah . . . I hadn't gotten that far . . . but it's not a bad idea."

Disappointed but wanting to be fair, he nodded in agreement. "I'll talk to my lawyer about it in the morning."

"So will I." Feeling deflated, she stepped back from him. "Do you want to go out to dinner?"

"Yes."

"I'll get dressed."

They walked out of the bathroom together. She turned toward her bedroom, then abruptly turned away and spun back around to face him. "I guess we've set ourselves quite a task."

He nodded. "We have. But I know I want us to live together and sort things out, not be apart."

She raised her eyebrows. "I don't think that's conducive to a celibate relationship."

"Neither do I." He grinned. "That's why I suggested it." He stepped closer to her and gazed intently at her. "I want to live with you, make love to you. What do you want?"

"I'm not sure." Myriad images of them together danced in front of her eyes. "It could be dangerous," she whispered.

"Granted. So? What do we do about that? I vote we live together."

"We could be hurt. I've been there. It's no picnic."

That jolted him. Did she mean she'd lived with someone before? "I've been stepped on a few times myself," he said, struggling to keep his voice even. "I didn't like it, but I prefer it to being frozen in nothingness."

She stared at him for long moments, then nodded once. "All right. We'll do it your way, trying to work things out before we make any sort of . . . final commitment. Okay?"

He loosed a silent sigh of relief.

"Okay."

"When?"

"Tonight. We'll dine, then come back here and get what you'll need for the next few days. Little by little, we'll move all your things over to my place."

"Oh?" She bristled, though she had the feeling

that Cullen wasn't trying to ride roughshod over her. "We've decided on your place, have we?"

He winced. "Sorry. I didn't mean to do that. My place is a large apartment. The whole third floor of Granger House. It's in the older section of Seattle near the water, but—"

"I know Granger House," she said. "You're some poor fisherman if you can afford that."

He nodded, his smile twisted. "I guess you do know the area. Granger House was one of the investments Gadsden and my father made. It was mostly Gadsden's idea. My father thought that having a small fleet of boats and going out for the catch was enough . . . and drinking a good portion of Irish whiskey to go along with it," he added wryly. "Gadsden likes to dabble in many things. He urged my dad to put up money, too, so they became joint owners of some fine real estate along the coast. It became a game to them."

Krystal chuckled, picturing the two friends speculating over land and house ventures. "They sound pretty shrewd."

"I suppose they were. Though I'd say Gadsden was the shrewder of the two. I can recall my father balking at some of the deals, arguing that they'd be better off hanging onto the cash."

"But then he'd change his mind."

"I guess so. They always seemed to go into a new venture." He shook his head. "They'd buy some properties in the older sections of towns and cities, not too run-down, then turn the larger single dwellings into condos or town houses and lease them. Smaller places, they'd renovate and sell or lease. They made as much money at that as they did at fishing."

"Enterprising, weren't they?" Krystal felt warmed by his telling her this. It helped her know him. "There must've been a great deal of mutual liking and respect."

"And several loud disagreements."

"What's wrong?" she asked when he suddenly looked surprised and pensive.

"I guess," he said slowly, "until we began talking, I'd forgotten the blowouts they used to have. Their arguing shook the rafters sometimes. My dad was always out on the boats, so I didn't see him as much as Gadsden after my mother died, but I can remember his temper. He let it fly at me a few times." He noted the small smile on Krystal's face. "What're you thinking?"

"I was just listening to you, thinking you had a good life out on the boats."

"I loved it." He paused, touching her cheek. "But weren't we talking about something else?"

"Yes."

"We were deciding about where to live. I can live here just as well."

She laughed. "You think so? We'd be slamming into each other all the time. And I don't have a surfeit of closet space." Her smile faded. "We'll try your place. Though I must be an idiot to leave here." At his quizzical look, she said, "It's nothing to do with you." She spread her hands. "It's so convenient. All I have to do is put a sign in the window that I'm closed and I can come up here and take a nap."

"And have you done that?" he asked, although

he already knew the answer to that. She was too damned hardworking to break for a nap.

"Not yet." But there was a measure of safety in having her own place, a place to run to and burrow in. Hiding would keep her from Cullen, though, and that'd be a bigger risk to her peace of mind.

He gently took hold of her arms. "If that's important to you, we'll leave most of your furniture up here and make it easy for you. What do you think?"

She nodded. "I'll try not to . . . hide from you." She smiled faintly. "I'm used to doing that, but I'm dealing with it."

He hugged her. "We'll be good together."

"We could be a mess."

"Pessimist. Let's go. I'm hungry."

"That's another thing. We have to share the chores." She laughed out loud at his grimace.

"You're stalling," he said. "Fine. We'll share the chores. I'm not much of a cook, but I can whiz through dishes, and I can corner sheets on the bed." He smiled at her triumphantly.

"Great. I'm a good chef. I'll do that, you clean up. I'll do the laundry, you can make the beds—"

"Bed. Mine's king-size." And having her in it was going to drive him wild. He'd never sleep. His whole being was aroused.

"Bed," Krystal repeated quietly, rocked by the vision of the two of them nestled together. "We'll talk on the way to the restaurant."

"If I have the strength," he muttered as she disappeared into her bedroom.

Six

Since Cullen was casually dressed, Krystal decided not to wear a skirt. She chose instead a pair of black wool pants and a cream-colored silk blouse.

"I'm ready," she told him when she returned to the front room. He'd been standing facing the bedroom door.

"So am I," Cullen said. He wasn't talking about dinner, and he knew she knew that. He could tell by the widening of her eyes, the shading of pink up her cheeks. He stretched out his hand. When she put hers into it, his heart cartwheeled. "I thought we'd go to Angelique's. You liked it there."

"Yes." And there'd been that lovely aura there, she mused, the beginning of knowing how much he meant to her. She wanted to be there with him again. She wanted to savor the memory, and the present.

Dinner was succulent. At least it looked that way to Cullen. He ate with gusto, but all his attention was on Krystal. Everything in the restaurant was perfect—their private corner table, the candlelight and soft music. But she was the star in his sky, and she blinded him to anything else.

They had almost the same food as they did that wonderful first evening, and Krystal reveled in the joy of it. Marvelous Pacific salmon in a creamy tarragon sauce; spinach salad with hot bacon dressing; fresh bread sticks, hot, crusty, yeasty, and fragrant with rosemary. Maybe she'd eat enough to fill out her clothes a little better, she thought.

"Very good," she said when she finished. She dabbed at her mouth with her ecru-colored linen napkin, then sat back, smiling. "I can never get enough of the wonderful West Coast fish. Salmon never tasted this good back east."

"Thank you, ma'am. We deliver to Angelique's, as well as some of the other best restaurants in the city." He grinned at her surprise. "We've quite a few contracts in the area, and this is one of the best for French cuisine. Let me order the dessert."

"Don't tell me you catch that too." She chuckled at his grimace. He was such fun. And he could laugh at himself. He'd told her hilarious stories about his misadventures on the boats.

"No," he said, but I do know Angelique's won a silver medal for this wonderful hazelnut confection called *torte de ciel*." He leaned forward when she licked her lips. "I wish you'd do that to me."

She blinked, her mind rolling back over what she'd done. Then she blushed fiery red. "Do you?"

"Very much. The thought of you licking my lips has me weak in the knees, Krystal Wynter."

"Ahh, a great discovery," she said lightly, trying

to keep the huskiness from her voice. "Now I know how to bring you to your knees."

"It's easy. Just look at me with those wonderful eyes and I'm on the floor." He stared at her. She was even more beautiful than when he'd first met her. "You're lovely," he said hoarsely, "and I'm a sucker for jade-green eyes."

"Thank you." She wanted to tell him that she thought he was beautiful, too, but the words couldn't get past her tight throat. She was caught in the throes of wild crosscurrents.

He lifted her hand to his mouth, never taking his eyes off her. Turning her hand over, he pressed his mouth to her palm, his tongue touching lightly. "You're in my blood, Krystal Wynter."

"Am I?" If he hadn't been holding her hand, she would have slipped under the table. His touch turned all her bones to soft wax.

Neither moved when the waiter wheeled the dessert cart over to them. The man had to cough twice to get their attention.

Cullen looked up, irritated. "Torte," he said, then looked back at Krystal.

She would have laughed, but she was too caught up in their private vortex.

She was sure she wouldn't be able to do the dessert justice, but when it was brought to her, her mouth watered. It was delectable and she ate most of it. Cullen finished hers as well as his own.

"Dance with me," he said as she sipped her coffee.

"All right."

Shaking with anticipation mixed with trepidation, she preceded him to the dance floor, threading her way through the tables. When she turned, he was there, taking her in his arms, making her melt.

"What are you thinking?" he asked, his lips brushing her hair.

"That I'm having a wonderful time," she whispered. She didn't mention that she was looking forward to later in the evening too. And her anticipation shocked her. Whenever she'd spent time with men, she'd avoided sexual confrontations, provocative talk, touching. Now she was pretty sure that if Cullen didn't suggest they spend the night together, she would.

"I'm having a good time too," Cullen murmured. He kissed her neck and felt her shiver. His own body quaked with want. He wanted to leave, take her to his place, and love her. Then he was damn well going to insist they marry, even with a prenuptial agreement. Admittedly that put a damper on things, but he wanted it if she did.

It had been his idea to have one dance, finish their coffee, and leave. But one dance led to another. Krystal was rhythmically perfect and fitted to him so well. She loved rock and danced to it with a restrained wildness that intrigued him, but she slow-danced so sweetly, too, he was loath to let her go.

When they finally returned to the table, their coffee was tepid. Neither wanted it.

"Shall we go?" Cullen asked, trying to read her expression. He didn't want to suggest or intimate anything that would send her screaming into the night.

She nodded, looking into his eyes. "I'm ready."

There was a sultriness to her tone and words, a sweet, soft heat that made his breath catch. "So am I," he said huskily.

"Then let's go." She reached out, smiling when he grasped her hand.

Cullen scrambled for his wallet with his free hand, not wanting to bother with the few minutes using a credit card would have entailed. He dropped several bills on the table, then snatched up their coats and led her out to the foyer. He paused long enough to help her with hers and shrug into his. When she chuckled, he glanced at her, smiling ruefully. "I'm trying not to hurry too much."

"Aw, go ahead and hurry." She laughed out loud at the long look he gave her.

"Having fun, are you?"

"Yes, indeed." And she was! She's never felt such a carefree happiness, such a sense of serenity.

They exited the restaurant arm in arm. It was a cold night, but there was more than a hint of spring mistiness in the air. Patches of ice still shone along the sidewalk, as though winter was being stubborn and couldn't make up its mind either to melt or freeze. The sky was crystal clear, onyx, and frosted with diamonds. A slice of moon glowed platinum.

Krystal inhaled and smiled. The night was magic.

Cullen put his arm around her, keeping her close to his side. It was unbelievably wonderful to hold her. They walked on to the car, eschewing the services of the valet, and they moved as one, happy, relaxed.

Once in the car, it all changed. Tension lassoed both of them.

Cullen cleared his throat. "Would you rather—"

"If you'd like to—"

They'd spoken at the same time. They glanced at each other sheepishly, then looked away.

Cullen started the engine, but didn't pull out into the street. "What do you want, Krystal?"

She took two deep breaths, exhaling slowly. "I—I want to go to your apartment. I've never been inside Granger House," she added lightly.

"Time you had a tour, then," he answered in the same vein, though his blood roared through him.

Now that they were driving to his place, Krystal wasn't able to keep the smile off her face. He wanted her. She'd heard it in his voice. That was happiness. She couldn't dredge up even a smidgeon of trepidation.

Cullen moved his hand from the gearshift to her lap, finding her hand and threading his fingers through hers. "You can always change your mind, and it'll be just fine."

She glanced at their clasped hands, then up to his face, and she squeezed his fingers. "I'm not afraid," she told him.

"I am," he said, and smiled when she laughed. "We're communicating so beautifully."

"We are." Taking a deep breath, she looked over at him. "You should know that you'll probably meet other people who attended Violet's parties, even here in Seattle." Just saying that dislodged some of her self-consciousness.

"Introduce me or don't," he said easily. "It'll be your choice. What they say, who they are, what business they're in will be immaterial to me as long as you're interested in me, not in them."

"I'm interested in you," she said, her voice barely audible.

"Good. I feel the same." He turned the car onto a narrow, hilly street paved with stones, then pulled over and parked. "We've arrived."

She looked at the honey-hued brick building with the cream-colored stucco trim and shook her head. "It's lovely and warm-looking, even on a cold night."

"Yes." He leaned closer and kissed her hair, inhaling the wonderful fragrance of Krystal Wynter. "There are five floors," he said. "I have the top floor. I was going to share it with Gadsden, but he prefers hotel living for the brief periods he's in Seattle. Of course, he likes California best of all."

"And Violet."

"What?" Enraptured by the sweet curve of her cheek, he didn't understand what she meant at first. Then he nodded, kissed her cheek, and got out of the car. He walked around to her side to help her out. Her hand trembled when he touched her, and he grinned. "I'm pretty shook up about this too. I think I want it too much."

She nodded. "I recall one Christmas Eve at my home in Lancaster. I thought the morning would never come. Then it did and the day flew by so fast, it was as though it hadn't happened." She smiled up at him. "After that I stopped wishing so hard for Christmas to come, and wished instead for it to be a very slow day."

He chuckled and curved an arm around her waist. After unlocking the two outer doors, he led her into the large foyer. A carousel couch sat in the middle of the foyer, upholstered in wine-colored taffeta. On the far side, wide stairs curved up to the second floor, the mahogany banister rising from an intricately carved pineapple newel post. Two elevators were set along the near wall.

"Very Victorian," she said. She loved the high ceilings, the wainscoting in deep mahogany that didn't look heavy, but graceful. There was quiet, dignity, and elegance, all in one delightful mix of the bygone era.

Cullen grinned. "Gadsden added all the little touches, like the lamps that look like gaslights, and the brass fans in front of the fireplaces. I should hate this foyer. I like plain. My boat is stripped to the boards. I sometimes summer in an Alaskan cabin that has only the barest essentials and I love it." He shrugged. "But when I come home to this, I feel *home.* Relaxed. Those outside walls are three feet thick and I never hear any traffic noise."

"Very nice." It was more than that, though, Krystal thought. It was a room, not a lobby. It would be good for meditating, for reading, for intellectual pursuits, as well as artistic ones.

They didn't have to wait for the elevator, and as soon as they stepped inside, he leaned down to kiss her on the mouth. She put a hand to his cheek, and he immediately deepened the kiss, his mouth opening over hers.

As though Cullen Dempsey were the answer to her prayers, she sighed with the pure joy of kissing him. She let her tongue touch his lips tentatively, then more assertively. As she took his tongue into her mouth, she swallowed his ragged gasp.

Holding each other, they swayed in the grip of a wondrous, deep, and satisfying pleasure that held them willing prisoners.

The wrought-iron filigree elevator doors made a muted clanging sound when they stopped. She reared back from him, startled.

"Damn doors," he said hoarsely. "Should have regular ones. Make too much noise."

"Not really," she said, her smile wobbling.

"I don't like anything disturbing us." Taking her hand, he led her from the elevator into a short hallway with two doors. He pointed to the far door. "When this was two apartments, that was Gadsden's door. But we renovated the two into one, and that became the kitchen door." Even as he spoke, he was concentrating more on the way her hair winged back form her forehead than on any floor plan.

"Oh." Krystal's brain had turned to mush. She couldn't think of anything to say to him. She wanted to be where she was, she looked forward to their passion, but at that moment, she couldn't relax with him. Why?

He kept her close to his side as he unlocked the door. "Enter," he said.

She smiled fleetingly and walked past him into the apartment. She stopped dead instantly, staring at the huge picture window across the room that revealed the panorama of Seattle at night. "Oh, how lovely." She stayed his hand when he would have pressed the light switch. "Don't. It's such a beautiful sight. You can see the harbor and the islands."

He nodded. "It's a good view on a clear day. And it has a special eerie wonder on the misty days. The first time I saw this place, I knew I wanted to live here. The previous owner had just left for a teaching job in Tokyo, so I didn't even have to ask anyone to leave."

She walked closer to the window, fascinated by the nocturnal mural, the kaleidoscope of lights, the scudding clouds, the glinting blue-white stars, the slice of moon with its silvery aura. "It's wonderful. I'd never turn on the lights."

"Fine with me." He moved behind her, sliding his hands around her waist and urging her back against him. His mouth trailed kisses along her neck. "I like staying this way." What an understatement, he thought. He'd never felt such fulfillment in his life, and they hadn't even made love yet.

Krystal turned her head, letting their mouths meet. Her heart beat out of rhythm at the sudden passion and fire, and at the rightness of it. She'd had a few different homes in her life, but never had she felt the sense of homecoming she was experiencing at that moment. It was as though all the odd pieces of her life had come together in one fell swoop, fitting, joining, and interlocking in one precious kiss.

He lifted his head. "I want you, Krystal. So very much."

"And I want you. But . . ."

"What is it?" He held his breath. If she backed out now, it would tear him apart, yet he had no intention of pressuring her. He wanted her as eager and willing as he was.

She turned fully in his arms, letting her hands slide up his chest and curl around his neck. "No doubt you're expecting an experienced woman—"

"I expect nothing from you." He kissed her nose. "And I have no preconceived notions about you. Though I freely admit I've been fantasizing about having you in my arms and in my bed since we met."

She tried to answer his smile with one of her own, but she failed. "Can I be serious for a moment?"

He nodded, then brushed a strand of hair from her cheek and kissed her. "I'm serious."

"I—I didn't go to bed with all those men in San Francisco. She gulped in a breath of air. It shouldn't have been difficult to tell Cullen such a thing.

"I never thought you did, Krystal. And, anyway, I don't give a damn. I love you. I would never sit in judgment on you."

Shaken, trembling, she gripped his shoulders as tears sprang to her eyes. "Thank—thank you."

"I mean it," he said, stroking her cheek.

"I believe you." She sighed raggedly. "Please let me finish." He nodded once more. "I haven't gone to bed with that many men." She shook her head. "No. That's not what I meant." She swiped at the perspiration on her upper lip. "I've never gone to bed with anyone," she said in a rush, then looked up at him, bracing herself.

"What?" Blood thrummed in his head, his heart stopped, his brain went on hold. She couldn't mean what she'd said.

"I'm not . . ." she stumbled on, "I haven't . . . There hasn't been anyone until you."

He stared at her. "Are you a virgin, darling?"

Miserably, she nodded. "And don't tell me I must be the oldest virgin on the face of—"

He kissed her, hard, then swung her up into his arms, his mouth still locked to hers. When he let her go they were both breathless. "Crazy lady," he murmured. "You've offered me a beautiful gift. Don't you know that?"

"You don't mind?" Reeling, she stared at his boyish smile, amazed by the pleasure beaming out of him.

"Don't be foolish," he chided gently. "You tell the man who loves you that you're a virgin, and you think you're going to get anger? Not so." He kissed her again, then lifted one hand and caressed her cheek. "To me you've always been untouched. I truly felt that way. And I never cared that you had other relationships. I've had them, and that's my past. I considered any men in your life as your past. Honestly, I didn't care, as long as you could come to love me now, and you'd let me be the last man in your life. I want that more than I can say."

"I want that too. I want to be your last woman." She shook her head. "I was so sure you'd think I was a little crazy. But I never met any man I wanted to share my passion with, so I saved it . . . for you, I guess."

"Oh, God, I love you." He caught her up in his arms again, letting her feet dangle above the floor. "I want to take you to bed."

"Yes." She pulled back a bit from him. "But you'd better be good at this, since you'll be my initiator."

"I promise to give it a hundred and ten percent," he said, laughing breathlessly.

"Good." She closed her eyes and clung to him, her mouth pressed to his neck.

"But I'm going to make a few requests myself," he added.

"What are they?" She looked around her as he carried her into the bedroom suite.

"Don't blow in my ear that way, or kiss me on the neck. I'll make a fool of myself before we get started." When she giggled and her breath touched him, he groaned. "Krystal!"

"I'm sorry," she said, eager and elated that she could arouse him.

"You don't sound it." He let her slide down his body, then gestured to the room. "Like it?"

"I love it." She felt his hands at her hair, pulling out the pins one at a time. She turned around and caught his hands. "Is this part of the ritual?"

"Yes. Do you mind?"

"No. But I'd like you to clue me in as we go along."

He chuckled. "Well, let's see. First, I'm glad you like our bedroom. But if there's anything you want to change, do it." Just don't leave it. He didn't dare verbalize the urgency in his soul.

"Thank you." Her voice trembled as he undid the top button on her blouse. She was nervous but eager, hesitant yet ready to fly.

"This is step two," he said. "One of the nicest things to do is undress your loved one."

"Oh. Do I do that too? I'm not totally unfledged, you know. I've read a few romances in my time." And now she was going to be in one.

"Ah, good. An intelligent woman. I like that. Yes, feel free to disrobe me anytime you feel so inclined." He prayed he wouldn't collapse to the floor when she touched him.

"Well, I'd better not visit you at the office then," she said.

Her mirth touched him like a sensual feather. His hands shaking, he unfastened the rest of the buttons on her blouse, then slipped it off her shoulders. Desire clenched inside him as he stared at her creamy skin, at her breasts, covered only by lace and satin. No precious gem or fine painting could rival her beauty.

When she was standing before him in only her panties and bra, he squeezed his eyes shut. "Darling, I never thought I'd say this, but it's very hard for me to look at you. We'd better get into bed."

"Wait," Krystal said, her hands lifting to the buttons on his shirt. "I'm enjoying myself." She stared at him, fascinated as she watched his aroused body clench in on itself. He was a tall, strong, well-muscled man, beautifully made. And he was hers now, as she was his. She felt a pleasurable possessiveness. All that marvelous masculinity was for her.

She smiled, feeling a sureness that was alien to her, but no less wonderful for that. She sighed contentedly. "It's funny," she murmured as she stripped his shirt off him. "I expected to feel embarrassed. I thought I'd be the one to close my eyes and try to hide, but I feel very good at the moment, and totally relaxed."

"I'm not," he said roughly, fisting his hands.

She leaned forward and kissed his bare chest, her lips puckering over his nipples. "Very nice."

"No more, Krystal." He tore off his pants and flung them over his shoulder, then reached for her.

She stepped back teasingly, openly assessing him. "My, you're a gorgeous man, Dempsey. Great body." She chuckled at his bewildered smile and tapped him on the chest. "But I knew that before you dropped your pants."

He groaned, then laughed. "What in hell did they put in your seltzer water?" His enjoyment and passion were enhanced by hers. Krystal wasn't intimidated or afraid. She wanted the lovemaking as much as he did. He swept her into his arms and strode to the bed. "You're a wild woman, do you know that?"

"I'm beginning to, Cullen Dempsey." She clung to him, burying her face in his neck, loving his masculine scent.

He sank down on the bed, still holding her tightly. She cuddled up against him, and his delight built, as though someone had handed him the firmanent for his own.

"Why did I ever think this would be a difficult experience for me?" she said. "I think I know instinctively what to do." She kissed him lightly.

"I think you do too."

She smiled at him, then wriggled free of his hold as they lay on the bed. Reaching behind herself, she unhooked her bra and slowly slipped it off.

"I'd do that," he said, watching her intently, "but I don't think it'd be a good idea. To tell the truth, I'm a little afraid to touch you." He'd never before felt such an overwhelming surge of desire and power. In all his life he'd never been so excited, nor so pleased, yet he wasn't even touching Krystal.

Krystal herself was having a marvelous time. No one had to explain why their movements were so liquid, so easy, with no trepidation, only curiosity, eagerness. Love was the emollient that smoothed things. Maybe Cullen didn't know that they really, truly loved, but she did. And she'd tell him, but not at the moment. She was too caught up in seducing him and being seduced. She was reveling in the first true self-confidence of her life. She was riding the rapids of the present and future on a raft of love and passion, and she could've screamed with the ecstasy of it. And there'd be more. Along the way she'd savor each tiny plateau, each wonderful nuance, each sweet expansion of feeling that would be theirs.

Cullen reached for her. "My lady," he whispered.

Seeing the passion in his eyes, she trembled. "A strange sensation, isn't it," she murmured, "to be together like this?"

"Yes." As she gazed at him, he wanted to grab her, throw her down on the bed, and kiss her senseless. But he'd promised himself he'd go slow with her.

"Oh, Cullen. It's so wonderful." She reached up and cupped his face in her hands. "I didn't know."

Groaning, he pulled her into his arms. He pressed his mouth to hers in a long, drugging kiss as he fell backward on the bed, taking her with him. His breathing ragged, he whispered, "Baby, neither did I."

They stripped and discarded what little clothing

was left on them. It took mere seconds for both to be naked. The dimly lit bedroom allowed them to see each other clearly, and they looked their fill.

"I'm in a damned hurry," he said, "but I don't want you to miss anything."

She smiled, bemused and delighted, as she stroked her leg up and down his, loving that furry abrasion on her skin. "Whatever." She grinned when she heard his throaty chuckle against her skin.

Slowly he feathered his hands up and down her thighs. When he heard her sigh, he kissed her neck. "So soft . . . but beautifully muscled too."

"All that scrubbing has paid off. Nothing more aerobic than cleaning a floor."

He chuckled as he slid down her body, until his mouth was pressed to the valley between her breasts.

Liking the sensation, she moved against his mouth. Nor could she stop from rubbing her legs against his hands. When his fingers roved over her, she writhed in agonized pleasure. A nub of heat had started at her core. It radiated outward, increasing, expanding. When he moved up her again and kissed her lips, then let his mouth once more range her upper body, she arched against him. In the whirling wonder of her mind she was shocked at how quickly rampant desire had seized her, yet she wanted it, needed it.

"Krystal," he whispered as he trailed kisses down her body.

Dazed, she reached out, grabbing his hair. "Cullen, I don't—"

"Shhh, darlin', easy. It's all right." He was stunned by the web of passion enclosing him, wild, wonderful, and exhilarating. He wouldn't have pulled back from her at that moment for anything in the world. She was heart, soul, and life to him.

"Should it be this good?" she asked on a moan.

"Yes, yes, it should." Her body quivered when his questing hands found the triangle of hair at the junction of her thighs. His fingers gently explored there, coaxing her wet heat, feeling the flowering, the welcoming.

Tremors shot through her until she was sure her bones would rattle with the intensity. When he lifted himself over her again and suckled at her breast, she cried out. Then lower, lower, his sensuous mouth touched every pore, burning her. Lower still, until he touched the core of her, and shock and passion had her calling out his name. A torrid rush suffused her. She had to be closer, to be fused to him.

Lifting her upward, he pressed his mouth there, repeating the wonderful cadence of the life pulse. The need to have her explode with sexual heat increased his passion a thousand fold.

He loved her with all that he was, his tongue flicking and probing, until he felt her stiffen. She tried to call out to him, but the ecstasy overwhelmed her. She gave herself over to it completely, and watching her, he nearly went up in flames himself.

"Cullen?" she finally murmured as he cradled her in his arms.

"Yes, love, I'm here." God, she was wonderful, he thought. Never had he experienced such all-encompassing loving. If truth be told, he hadn't realized there was such a thing. She'd taken him to new planets, untouched territories of sensations, unplumbed depths of feeling. She hadn't held back one piece of herself.

Now, he'd initiate her into their ultimate togetherness. Passion warred with nerves—it had to be good for her! He positioned his body over hers.

When she would have clutched him to her, he gently loosened her hands. Then he edged against her into the opening, taking deep breaths to still his thundering heart. Easing into her, he found the barrier, and felt an almost infinitestimal stiffening on her part before she forced herself to relax. He tried entry again, and her tight wetness made him want to plunge into her, hard and deep.

But he saw how she squeezed her eyes shut, as if expecting pain. No pain for you, my love, he promised silently. He eased away from her, and her eyes snapped open.

"What's wrong, Cullen?"

"Nothing, love." He kissed her gently, nibbling on her lower lip. "Everything is perfect."

"Then why . . . ?"

"I'm loving you." Before she could respond, he moved down her body, kissing his way over the creamy skin that bloomed hot with passion, igniting his libido anew. When he reached that wonderful junction of her body, he felt her arch in surprise.

"I thought we were done," she said shakily.

"Just beginning." Blood thudded through him. He longed to taste her once more.

Lifting her hips, he pulled her against his mouth. Her body arched again. He heard her questioning moan, but he didn't release her. Instead he began an age-old rhythm that had her writhing and plunging beneath him. When she cried out, surging against him, her body shuddering in beginning culmination, he surged up and entered her.

He tried to be gentle, but she wouldn't let him. Clutching him to her, she wrapped her legs around him. She felt a sudden tearing, a sting, but she was so caught up in the sensual delight that it didn't register.

Groaning, Cullen gave in to her demands and took her fully, even as she took him.

Spun out of control, they whirled through rapture to the world where only lovers go. They hung suspended there, caught in the wonderful grasp of romantic love.

"I didn't know," she whispered.

"Darling, neither did I."

"Will we always have it?"

"Always."

Seven

Warm days and hot nights draped themselves over the new lovers, even as Seattle, in early spring, was still caught in blasts of cold from Mt. Olympus to Mt. Rainier. The heat was their own, and they generated it with a look, a touch, a smile. Even the signing of the silly prenuptial agreement didn't dampen their ardor.

The days and weeks that followed that first night were euphoric, incredible, cataclysmic . . . scary. It hadn't seemed possible, yet now it was here. To Krystal their happiness had an almost unreal quality. She was sure it could and would end at any moment. Not all of her joy could mitigate all of her fear.

Even now, six weeks after they'd begun living together, she couldn't bring herself to believe in the future. She could only take it one day at a time. Late one afternoon, Krystal stared out the window of her store, its black letters announcing that

Wynter's could clean anything, gleaming silver in the sunlight. Everything was prepared for the night shift, and as usual when she had a few free moments, she was daydreaming about Cullen.

When the phone rang, she jumped. "Hello."

"Hello, sweetie. It's Violet. I'm happy to announce Gadsden and I will be coming to Seattle in little more than a week. One of those fund-raiser things, I think. But I'll get to see you, because Gadsden says you and Cullen will be joining us."

"Great. I can't wait to see you." Had Cullen mentioned it? she wondered.

"Are you happy, Krystal?"

"Yes."

They talked for a while. When she hung up, Krystal felt guilty. She'd heard the puzzlement in Violet's voice when Violet had asked if she was happy. Intuitive as always, she'd picked up on Krystal's uncertainty.

She mentioned the call to Cullen while they were still lying in bed the next morning, replete from glorious lovemaking.

"Yes," he said, "We'll be seeing them. I should give you my calendar so I don't forget to tell you things."

She laughed. "Sometimes we're concentrating on other things."

"Yes." He kissed her neck, his mouth roving over her satiny skin. She clung to him languorously. "So," he murmured, "do you want to continue living here at Granger House?"

"I like it here," she said, her voice still husky and love-filled. "The bed is big . . . and that's what counts." Without opening her eyes, she smiled in response to his chuckle.

"True." He kissed her again, then sighed. "I have to go. I have an important meeting this morning."

She yawned hugely, nodding. "You should go."

"Right." He kissed her stomach, liking the way it clenched in on itself at his touch. "Damn! I don't want to go."

"You never do. And I never want you to." She shrugged one bare shoulder. "What can we do?"

He kissed her hard and rolled away from her. "Live on a deserted island." He grumbled when she laughed. "Are you working tonight?"

She nodded reluctantly. "I think I should. Plotnitz is ill again, and it's too much for the skeleton crew to handle."

"I'll join you when I'm done at the office. Keep an open mind to Chinese food."

"I always have an open mind to Chinese. I love the stuff." She rolled out of bed, sated and happy, and stretched.

"Dammit, don't do that," Cullen muttered, turning away.

Showering together was a mistake, making parting even more difficult. Dressing was an ordeal they faced every day. Neither could look away from the other.

"We should have separate rooms," Cullen said grimly. "And if I could bear it, we would. I like that suit," he added. "You look wonderful in it, businesslike and sexy."

"Isn't that a contradiction in terms?"

"Not in your case. Have to run." He kissed her and bolted for the door.

Krystal was whistling to herself as she walked out of Granger House to her van. No longer rusted and unwieldy, it stood proudly with a new paint job and shiny chrome. It ran now like a sweetly oiled machine. Cullen had seen to that. She'd balked when he'd tried to insist on a new van. Her good Mennonite background rebelled at such waste.

It wasn't that far from Granger House to her place, and as usual she enjoyed the early-day bustle of Seattle. Though she could have gone a less-traveled route, she drove the busier way past The Market. There was something magical about it in the morning. Even on cold, rainy days, she would roll down her window to inhale the myriad smells. And she did so that morning. The acrid, fishy odor superimposed over all the other fragrances might have been anathema to some, but to Krystal it was perfume. She'd come to love Seattle—the people, the climate, the ambience. And now she'd stay, with Cullen.

She pulled her van into the narrow driveway beside her building, drove to the back, and parked. After locking the door, she hurried into her shop, away from the bite of a strong morning breeze. As usual it was chilly inside, because she'd gotten into the habit of turning the heat down before leaving for home. She was too frugal to leave it on. As she turned up the thermostat, she noticed the message light was flashing on her answering machine. She groaned silently and prayed she didn't have another sick employee.

She pressed the button, listening to the messages as she straightened up the desk.

The first was from a part-time worker who said

he could come in that evening. The second message was from Plotnitz, telling her he was much better and would be on the job that night. Things were definitely looking up; it was a good beginning to the day.

The third message made her drop her pencil and sink into the desk chair, staring at the wall with the framed copy of Winslow Homer's "Girl Carrying a Basket." She didn't see the girl balancing her burden on one hip. She saw nothing, felt nothing, but then pain began to knife through the numbness. For a moment she thought she'd lose her light breakfast of oatmeal and skim milk. Then the churning stopped. Her lawyer, kindly Mr. Duval, had blown her world apart. The message said it was about the prenuptial agreement. Mr. John Banks, Cullen's lawyer, had called him about amending paragraph six. Would she call Mr. Duval? The agreement! she thought, bewildered. They'd had their lawyers draw it up, they'd signed it, and then they'd promptly forgotten it. At least she had.

She dialed the attorney. "Mr. Duval, please. Krystal Wynter calling." Her voice had a hollow sound. "Hello. I received your message. Yes, I understand. No, I don't want you to tell him that. I'll sign it . . . and I'll do it today." She hung up the phone even as he protested, then leaned back in the chair, shaking.

Myriad thoughts threw themselves around her brain as though they rode a fast roller coaster. Nothing made sense, yet it did. Coldly and implacably, it came together. Fear and grief coiled in her, but she ignored them. Be rational, practical, she told herself. But fear blocked any attempt to soothe the pain.

She called for an appointment with John Banks, then forced herself to get to work. At lunchtime she ignored her usual fare of skim milk and fruit yogurt, closed up the shop, and walked out back to her van. This time she didn't notice its gleaming fresh paint.

Pain was her passenger during the circuitous ride to the law firm, whose offices were close to the Hall of Justice. She took the elevator to the tenth floor, then stepped out into a richly appointed reception area. The offices of Banks, Banks, Lieval and Dorn were subdued, mauve, and surrounded by quiet baroque music. On one wall, an abstract avant-garde pen and ink drawing offered a sharp contrast to the serenity.

"I'm Krystal Wynter," she told the well-groomed receptionist. "I have an appointment with—"

"Of course. Mr. Banks is waiting for you. Just through those double doors to the left." The smiling woman with the platter-sized glasses pressed a button, and the doors opened with a swish.

An acre of mauve carpet stretched from the door to a white oak, kidney-shaped desk. Twin deep mauve-upholstered chairs faced the man who rose, smiling tightly at her, one hand outstretched.

"I'm Krystal—"

"Wynter. Of course. I'm John Banks, Cullen's attorney. I was told you were quite attractive. I can see it was an understatement."

His smooth attempt at flattery grated on her like sandpaper, but she tried to smile.

The walk to the upholstered chairs took forever.

The only sound in the room was the whir of the pencil sharpener when Banks put in a pencil with his left hand. His right hand was still held out to her. Perversely, she hurried to clasp his hand while he was still sharpening the pencil, and tugged ever so gently. When he seemed to lose his balance, tipping toward the desk, she smiled. Now she didn't feel like the only one off keel.

Frowning slightly, Banks gestured her to sit in one of the chairs across from him, then reseated himself, clasping his hands in front of him on the desk. "Now. As you know, Ms. Wynter . . . Or do you prefer Miss?" He cocked his head in a birdlike fashion and waited. "Of course, I can call you Krystal." His laugh was feathery, breathy.

"Ms. Wynter is fine," Krystal said, dry-mouthed. Dreading to hear what this prim and prunelike man had to tell her, she stared unblinkingly at him.

"Well, I must say," he began, "I don't generally act as your . . . ahem, as Mr. Dempsey's attorney." He coughed behind his hand. "My father, James Banks, represents your . . . ah, Mr. Dempsey, and some of the other more lucrative . . . er, ah, that is, there's been an error. A new clerk mixed up the folders and I have Mr. Dempsey's in front of me." He opened it, rattling some of the papers as he perused them. "I see no problem with this. It's relatively easy to handle. So, I decided to relieve my father of some of his burdensome cli— That is, not that the client is burdensome. But with something this simple, I can do it. Not that I don't handle more involved—"

"I get the picture, Mr. Banks," Krystal said

tightly. "Shall we get on with it?" She threaded her fingers together and tried to keep from screaming. *Damn you, Dempsey!* she cried silently. *You let me love you. Why? Why?*

Banks stared at her for a moment, wrinkling his nose like a rabbit. "Yes. Well." He cleared his throat, and tapped the papers in front of him, staring down at them through his half glasses. "Though this is a simple procedure, it should be done right, and I wrote this most carefully so there'd be no cause for action . . . that is, errors in the future." Pursing his lips into a tight bow, he glanced at her once more, then began to read, methodically, ponderously, every word clearly enunciated.

"I understand the agreement, Mr. Banks," Krystal said, interrupting him halfway through. "I have a copy and I've read it." And yet, because it hadn't been mentioned between them since they'd signed it more than a month ago, she'd thought the whole matter had been dropped. She'd been glad to kick it out of her mind. It was a kick in the head, instead, to find that Cullen meant to pursue it with the same gusto and strength of purpose he put into his career.

"Fine, fine," Banks said. "Well, I've made a few changes, for the good of the client, as you might understand, but it's pretty straightforward." He looked at her challengingly. She gazed back in silence, and he glanced down again, clearing his throat once more. "I contacted your lawyer yesterday and insisted that paragraph six must be amended. He balked. But I will tell you, as I told him, that I intend to stand firm on this point."

"Go on." She didn't like the look on Banks's face. All she wanted to do was sign the damn thing and leave.

Then she was going to get her things from Granger House and move back to her apartment above the store. She couldn't deal with Cullen going behind her back like this, his obvious lack of faith in her.

"Ms. Wynter, this is an old and honorable law firm. It wouldn't serve our clients' best interests if we didn't protect them as best we could—"

"Get on with it." The words were torn from a throat raw with unshed tears.

"Very well," Banks said huffily. "It's come to my attention that you were involved in a scam of some sort in San Francisco, Ms. Wynter. You must understand our position in trying to protect our client. Therefore, we've written a codicil to the agreement that you receive nothing if the relationship lasts less than five years. After that, if something goes wrong, you'll get a fair and equitable settlement, as my client has stipulated." Banks closed the folder with a snap and pushed a single sheet of paper toward her. "Under no circumstances will you take over Dempsey Fisheries, no matter what the occurrence. Sign at the bottom, if you please."

Krystal signed, took her copy, and rose.

"I trust there'll be no hard feelings, Ms. Wynter. Business is business."

Banks's chuckle died when she stared stonily at him. Without saying a word, she turned and walked out, slamming the door behind her.

Krystal didn't know how she got home without

getting into an accident. She went up to the apartment and packed like an automaton, taking only what she'd need for the next few days. She could get her other things at a later date.

You betrayed me, Cullen! the negative voice in her head screamed. *You told me you thought me* *clear of the nasty gossip. You lied. I want to hate* *you.*

Krystal, you're a fool, her sane, more rational voice said. *You're running again, just as you did* *two years ago.*

I can't stay. I'll bleed to death if I do.

What good did it do to run before?

I love Cullen, but he can't love me or he wouldn't be doing this. Better a quick break than the death of a thousand days.

Trust him.

I can't. I want to, but I can't.

Maybe that prunelike Mr. Banks made a mis-take.

No, I did.

Just the bare necessities, she told herself over and over, not glancing at Cullen's razor or his toothbrush. She saw a dot of toothpaste they'd missed during their hurried cleanup before leaving the apartment. They always lingered too long in bed. It was agony to stare at the spot.

Finally done, she dragged two bulging suitcases, loaded with useful and useless paraphernalia and clothes, to her van. Why had she brought one of the new magazines from the coffee table? she wondered. She'd packed like a crazy woman.

She drove back to the store and toted the suit-cases to the upstairs apartment in a semicomatose condition. Standing inside the entryway after dropping her bags, she stared around her as though she'd never seen the place before. She shivered at its stark emptiness. Oh, the furniture was still there, the curtains were on the windows, but there was a dry, dusty echo to the rooms. The sound of loneliness. She shook her head, as though she'd drive the bogeys from her being. Then she walked around, opening the windows to freshen the air.

In harum-scarum fashion she unpacked, hung her clothes, and tossed her toiletries into the bathroom. Don't look back, she told herself. Fight back by succeeding. Revenge yourself by living well. All the axioms she'd flagellated herself with when she'd first come to Seattle had a bitter taste now.

After closing the windows, she took one last look at the neat but uninspiring apartment, then left. Downstairs the message light was flashing on the answering machine. As she was looking at it, the phone rang.

She neither turned on the machine nor answered the phone. Instead she went right to work, calling the late-shift forewoman and informing her that she'd be working with the crew that evening.

She drove across the city, feeling queasy as she approached her destination. Thank heavens it wasn't Cullen's building. She parked her van in the underground garage, then trudged to the cheerless custodial locker room.

One of her managers, Plotnitz, was there, and he looked at her in surprise. "Why you here, boss lady? Alma told me you were coming. We got enough staff tonight."

"How are you feeling?" Krystal asked, ignoring his question. Plotnitz was one of the first people she'd hired after starting the business, and she relied on him to oversee the jobs. They were rarely on the same assignment, and she knew he'd be puzzled and curious. She smiled blindly at his narrow-eyed scrutiny.

"I'm good," he said. "Som'pen wrong, boss lady?"

"Headache," Krystal said.

"Rough."

Plotnitz was going to say more, but she forestalled him by excusing herself and rushing to the supply closet. She made a noisy, confused job of retrieving gear, banging down equipment, and donning coveralls and work shoes. She almost sobbed with relief when her foreman walked away without saying more.

Two hours later, she was deep into floor scrubbing. It was a favorite way for her to work off her emotional tension, and she welcomed the swinging rhythmic motion that would make her shoulders ache in the morning and her knees feel numb. She gripped the mop as though it were her last anchor to earth.

She heard the swish of the elevator doors opening, but didn't look up. Everyone had assigned duties. There was little time for chitchat.

At first she didn't even notice his presence. Then she felt him, as though he'd entered her being and tapped her shoulder from the inside. Cullen! She knew it as surely as if he'd trumpeted his name, but didn't raise her head. "Yes?" Her voice cracked.

"What the hell is going on, Krystal?" Anger vibrated in his voice. "And don't pretend you don't understand."

She considered doing just that, but his words were like spears. He was past angry! The nerve of the man. Wasn't she the one who'd been suckerpunched? She set her mop in the bucket and propped it against the wall. Taking several deep breaths, she straightened and faced him. "I certainly don't understand your temper tantrum." She looked directly into his eyes, then was sorry she did. His eyes were fathoms deep with liquid fire.

"What the hell does that mean?" he asked, hands on his hips. "I come home, expecting to find a loving note from my lady, inviting me to a tête-à-tête in an empty building while she worked. Instead I find that she's removed a bunch of her clothes and personal things from our home. And there's no note, no explanation."

"Perceptive, aren't you? Did you count the silver?" She swallowed, hoping to steady her voice. At that moment she was a volcano about to erupt, and it wouldn't take much to set her off.

"Stop it." Anger whipped the words from his mouth. "Tell me."

"I just decided not to live with a man who doesn't trust me," she said tautly. His mouth dropped open, and she would've laughed if she hadn't been so caught up in wrenching ire.

"What harebrained notion brought you to that conclusion?"

"Don't you call me harebrained!" she bellowed, bringing one of her workers on the run.

"You okay, Miss Krystal?" Angel Torres asked, brandishing his vacuum cleaner wand.

"I'm fine, Angel. Go ahead and finish the far office. I'll join you in a moment."

"Okay. But I'm right here, if you need me." Angel glared at Cullen.

Both Krystal and Cullen were silent as Angel walked away, his foam-soled shoes thunking softly on the floor.

"I suggest," Cullen said at last, his voice deceptively soft, "that you don't involve anyone else in this little discussion of ours." His teeth cracked together for emphasis.

"Don't you come on like that. I won't take it from you, any more than I'd take it from those macho jerks who tried sexual blackmail on me in California." She shook her fist in his face.

Cullen went rigid. "Who? I want names." He'd kill the bastards, then he'd try to get Krystal to talk sense.

Suddenly her meaning struck him, like a blow to the chest. "You're comparing me to them?"

"Forget it. It's history," she muttered. "It's immaterial."

"The hell it is. You're part of my life, as I'm part of yours. I want to know about anyone who tried to intimidate you in any way—"

"Then you'd better get after yourself," she blurted out. "Nothing is more intimidating than being told that your past life precludes certain treatment in a prenuptial agreement—"

"What?"

"Don't you shout like that. You know what I'm talking about, Mr. Dempsey. Your watchdog was protecting your interests in case we break up, which we will be doing—"

"The hell we will!" Cullen roared, emptying offices up and down the hall as workers rushed out to see what was wrong.

"Stop roaring like a wounded bull," she shouted at him, then waved her reluctant workers back to their jobs. "You'll set off an alarm . . . or something."

"Ridiculous," Cullen said in a lower tone. He was silent for a minute. "Why did you go?"

"I thought it would be better, considering—"

"Considering what? What in hell is all this about that damn agreement? I'm not leaving here until you tell me."

She leaned down and picked up her bucket, running a practiced eye over the well-traveled area in front of the water fountain and elevator. They looked good. Generally there were scuff marks in those places that required extra time. "Come with me."

Cullen walked behind her, admiring the movements of her slim body, despite the coveralls. Krystal was beautiful even when she was wearing something so shapeless and unattractive. He followed her into an office and closed the door. She stopped in front of the desk and turned to face him. He went right up to her, his hands going to her waist. She pushed his hands away, but he didn't step back.

"Tell me," he said.

"I had a meeting today with Mr. John Banks of

Banks, Banks, Lieval and Dorn. He told me that they had to keep your best interests in mind, and he had therefore amended paragraph six of our agreement. He said it was because of my unsavory past—"

"Wait a minute! You're all wrong on this, Krystal—"

"No, I'm not. I signed the amendment today." She took a deep breath. "But I've decided that I don't want to live with a man who trusts me so little that—"

"So you'd walk rather than sit down and talk it over. Is that it?"

Why tell him about the flood of tears in her being? "Yes."

"Well, I'm sorry you feel that way, but I've got rights too. You can't kick me out without a hearing—"

"I didn't kick you out. I left. I'm back in my own place—"

"And that's where I'll be tonight and every night you are." Not giving her a chance to reply, he whirled and strode out of the office, slamming the door behind him.

"Cretin," she muttered to the empty room.

Voices echoed through her head for the rest of the night. He'd be at her apartment. He wouldn't. He was a louse. Maybe she should've listened to him. Nonsense. He was the one who'd instructed his lawyer. Perhaps talking it over with him might clarify a few things. Never.

Bone-tired, she washed and put away her equipment, checked out the last of the workers, and made her way down to the basement. She didn't relish going into the darkened parking garage. Cautious as always, she carried the atomizer filled with ammonia. When she heard a sound, she turned. She saw a hulking figure and sprayed.

"Dammit to hell! Krystal! My eyes . . ."

"Cullen? Oh my, I thought you were an intruder." She winced as he bent over, hands pressed to his eyes. "That must sting."

He coughed violently. "Trust you to act first and think later." As astringent and acrid as the sensation was, Cullen was glad Krystal could defend herself. But he was still furious with her for running out on him. Since he'd left her, he'd gone over what she'd told him, and was angered that she had so quickly believed the worst about him. He'd tried to get in touch with Banks, but the man wasn't at his office or home.

He felt her take his arm as he wiped his streaming eyes. She led him to the door to the custodian's locker room. "Hang on while I unlock this," she said. "Water will help. I'm sorry."

"Are you sure it's not acid?" he asked. His eyes still stung so badly, he couldn't open them.

"You're just being testy."

"Testy? Me? You just bombarded me with ammonia, and I'm testy? Dammit, Krystal." If it was his last earthly act, he was going to make her understand everything. And it might be. She was lethal.

Krystal got the door unlocked and led him inside. In the glare of a yellow wall lamp, she got a good look at him, and flinched. "Your eyes are a bit red . . . and swollen," she whispered.

"Well, hell, I can tell that. You could've blinded me, woman."

"Don't exaggerate," she mumbled. Feeling guilty, she soaked her clean hankie in cold water and began to dab at the area.

"Ouch! Krystal, that hurts. Oww. Easy."

She leaned back. "Don't be a baby."

"You weren't on the receiving end of ammonia, Krystal," he snapped at her.

"See. You're testy."

"Dammit, Krystal, it hurts."

"Well, you can't think I did this to you on purpose."

"I can't? After what you pulled today, I can."

She stared into his eyes for a moment, her resolve swaying. Then she shook her head. "I believe what's in black and white."

"So do I. And I also believe in what we've said to each other." He took her arm. "We're getting out of here. You drive. I'll pick up my car when I can see again."

Alarmed, she whirled to face him. "Maybe we should see a doctor. I'll take you to the hospital—"

"You'll take me home, wherever you're living. Let's go."

"You can't stay at my place. It's too small."

"I'll fit," he told her. Still holding her arm, he directed her into the passenger's side of the van, so that she had to climb over the console to get into the driver's seat.

"This is a bit awkward, isn't it?" she asked, frowning at him as he climbed in behind her.

"I'm not talking any chances you'd boot out of

the parking garage without me if I let you get behind the wheel first."

Affronted, she glared at him as she started the engine. "I happen to be a very caring person, Cullen Dempsey, and I wouldn't—"

"Sure, that's why you left me high and dry, without so much as a note."

"I explained that," she told him loftily.

"Like hell you did, but you will."

"Don't you threaten me, Cullen Hughson Dempsey."

"I'm not, and you know it, and stop calling me by my full name, like you're reading an indictment."

"Maybe I am."

Eight

Hell Week!

The five days following her moving back into the small apartment over her store couldn't be described any other way.

Cullen moved in with her, sleeping on the hide-a-bed in the front room. Within a day the place was a mess, a caldron strewn with clothes, bedding, papers, dirty dishes, empty cartons from take-out places. She cooked apathetic meals for herself. He relied on take-out. Tamari sauce odors mingled with cold, acrid jalapeño; sweet and sour warred with sushi. Though they constantly picked up, the place remained a shambles.

"Eating junk food won't add to your efficiency on the job," she told him one evening, holding at arm's length an empty carton that had contained fries.

"Being a shrew will only get you an acid stomach," he shot back, snatching the carton from her and feeling a black satisfaction when color stained her neck and cheeks.

"If I'd known you'd smoked," she said haughtily, "I wouldn't have considered living with you." Liar, she thought. She'd have crawled on her knees across the Pacific to be with him.

"If I stay with you," he said, stomping to the bathroom, "I'll have to give up tobacco and switch to opium."

"I'm not a shrew," she whispered to the closed bathroom door. She had to forcibly stop herself from picking up his beautiful gray worsted suit from where it lay in a heap on the floor. Let him take care of it.

He refused to share her closet. The only other place to hang anything was on hooks just inside the door in the tiny foyer. More than one of his fine silk and cotton shirts was draped there. The place was a war zone.

The kitchen was the worst. They didn't eat together because they rarely were home at the same times. If anything, they seemed more isolated each day, as Cullen left in the morning before she woke, and she purposefully worked every night—even though she didn't need to—not coming home until long after he'd gone to bed.

"I hate clutter," she said waspishly one evening before she left, then could've bitten through her tongue. What she meant was, I hate our estrangement.

"So do I," Cullen responded. "I'll order a garbage scow to back up to the door and we'll toss it all out the window." He meant, I don't care how I live if you don't love me. But I won't let you go.

"Do that." Throw everything out, she said silently. But not me, Cullen. Not me.

She did hate the clutter, but she knew what she hated more. She hated dreading the day Cullen would tell her that he was moving back to Granger House. She'd die then. She'd had ample time to ponder her impulsive move out of his place, and to question the words of John Banks, who was not really Cullen's attorney. If only she'd talked to Cullen first, maybe she wouldn't be so tongue-tied with him now. If only she could find the words to approach the burning subject that she'd made too hot to handle, maybe they could get over this hump of noncommunication.

The next evening she didn't dress for work. Cullen stared at her. "Are you ill?"

She shook her head. Exhausted was more like it. And tired of hiding. She'd decided earlier that day that it was long past time that she and Cullen talk. But how should she begin? "Did you know Gadsden and Violet will be here in a few days?" she asked, timidly choosing a roundabout approach.

He nodded. "I thought they could stay at Granger House."

"Then I should call Violet—"

"I talked to Gadsden," he said. Her eyes widened at his harsh tone. She had beautiful eyes, he thought. He wanted their heat all over him. His body hardened, and he had to force the sensual images away. The strain made his voice even harder. "He is my partner. I speak to him most days."

"Of course," she said coolly.

"They like Granger House," he added, his tone softer.

"Yes. Are there any empty apartments?"

"I offered them our place."

"You did?" Horrified, she stared at him. "What did they say?"

"Thank you," he said dryly. "If you're worried about what they may think, don't. They only know that we've moved here."

"And they have to wonder about that."

He shrugged. "So? Let them." He grabbed his jacket and arched a brow at her. "Do you want me to get you some take-out?"

"No, I thought I might make a pesto—"

"Fine. I'll get out of your way." He pulled on his jacket, grabbed his keys, and left.

"I was going to say," she said softly, "I had enough for two." She walked into the tiny kitchen and went about her chores blindly. The only part she enjoyed was crushing the garlic. The strong fragrance penetrated her misery, and she could think of something besides Cullen. He'd insisted, since they'd first begun dating, that they both eat garlic when it was served, so that one wouldn't be repelled by the other. Perversely, Krystal added two cloves instead of one.

The phone rang as she put on the pot for the pasta.

"Oh, Violet. Good to hear from you. We're looking forward to seeing you." Using the excuse that she was in the middle of dinner, Krystal cut the conversation short. Violet was sharp. She'd notice the tension between Krystal and Cullen right away. There'd be puzzlement, then inquiring looks. Krystal shuddered and leaned over the sink, quite sure she was going to be sick. The queasiness passed, though, and she straightened, inhaling deep breaths.

"What is it?"

She jumped at Cullen's sharp voice. "I didn't hear you come in. Did you forget something?"

"No. Something's wrong. What?"

She hesitated, then shrugged. "Violet just called. She and Gadsden will be arriving on schedule."

He frowned. "I knew that. What made you sick just then?"

"I wasn't sick. Just thinking about the tension that'll be around when they come is enough to make anyone queasy."

He shook his head. "That's not what made you ill. Something made me come back. I just knew something was wrong. You're pregnant, aren't you?"

"What?" She stared at him. "I certainly am not."

"You are. And you're hiding it from me, and now you want to leave me. What the hell is going on?"

"Nothing." She gasped when he all but lifted her off the floor and pulled her against his chest. "Stop it. Let me go."

"Never." He cradled her against him. "You're crazier than hell, and I'll never understand you, but I'm not letting you go. We're having this baby together."

"There's no baby," she told him, grinding her teeth when her body betrayed her at his touch. Her nipples hardened, her knees liquefied, her breathing turned shallow.

"It's not the prenuptial agreement that's turned you loony," he whispered against her hair. "You're expecting our first baby." He ran one hand up and down her back, his heart thudding against his breastbone. A baby! A girl like Krystal with wide-apart green eyes, a sweet smile, and a sparky temper.

"It's the agreement," Krystal said, trying to fight back against the melting of her being, the urge to embrace him.

"No. You're afraid to have the baby. I'll be here with you—"

"Cullen, I'm not the crazy one, you are."

He leaned back a fraction. "No. You wouldn't make such a fuss about something you suggested in the first place, something so unimportant to us." He pushed back the hair that had fallen forward on her cheek.

She stared at him while his words reverberated in her head. It wasn't important! He'd said it. Elation filled her, but was quickly submerged by guilt and regret.

"I'm not having a baby, Cullen," she said softly. "And I think we might have rushed things, not talked enough." He took a step back from her, and she instantly felt bereft. "We have a communication gap as wide as the Grand Canyon," she added, attempting some humor.

He didn't smile. "Explain," he said tersely.

She nodded slowly. "When I proposed the agreement, I—I guess I didn't think you'd agree to it—"

"You wanted it."

"I know, I know." She turned away from him. "I thought I was beyond my . . . past."

"You don't have one," he said abruptly.

She looked over her shoulder, trying to smile.

"We all have pasts. And . . . I thought I'd begun to put mine in perspective, that what had happened couldn't hurt me any longer. I was wrong. It still does. And down through the years, there will always be someone who will say something, who will bring it up, directly or by innuendo. I'm not sure I can handle it. Someone will remember—"

"Remember what? You did nothing. You're not responsible for your father's deeds. That he compromised you and Violet by letting certain people think you'd party with business acquaintances is his sin, not yours." Cullen frowned, certain she wasn't being completely frank with him. "Krystal, look at me. I'm not going to let you blame me for what your father did, either. That had nothing to do with what we are or what we have. Any agreement we sign is not running our lives. It works or it doesn't, based on what we do and say, how we feel. And I'm not letting you go until I know it's what you really want."

Silence.

"Tell me what you think," he said quietly.

Fatigued, drained, she looked up at him. "Right now I don't know what I think," she said, shrugging helplessly. "I don't seem to be able to sort it out."

He took hold of her upper arms. "Then let's not. We'll wait until after Violet and Gadsden leave, then we'll take it apart, brick by brick, and examine everything. Deal?"

Relieved not to have to face it until then, she nodded. "All right. We won't do any more until after Gadsden and Violet return to San Francisco."

"And we'll stay here and let them have the

apartment at Granger House . . . for now." Cullen freely admitted to himself that he intended to drive her into a corner any way he could. He cursed his own stupidity that he hadn't seen her vulnerability sooner. Dammit, she'd run from it, hadn't she? And she'd been innocent. No one knew that better than she. But either she hadn't thought herself worthy, or she was positive no one would believe her. She'd run, rather than face them down. Just as she'd tried to run from him. That was going to end.

She smiled faintly. "Cramped as it is, we'll stay here."

"Good." He leaned down and kissed her nose. "You don't know it yet, lady, but you're going to get rid of all your bogeys forever."

The next morning, two days before the fund-raiser, Krystal woke early. Even still, Cullen had gone already. Disappointment and frustration ate at her. They hadn't slept together since she'd left Granger House. In their six weeks there, their lovemaking had become essential. Even if he just walked in front of her, her blood thudded through her, and her desire seemed almost palpable. But with their relationship so unstable, how could she communicate her need to him? Cullen, dear, would you mind if I jumped your bones? Wonderful.

Annoyed with herself, she left the cloying confines of the apartment and went down to the office. Fortunately she was just about caught up in her paperwork, with only an hour of bookkeeping to finish. She typed out some items and instructions for the coming night and the next day, tidied up, and left.

Taking her van, she drove aimlessly, no destination in mind. Not far from Granger House was a little street of shops and boutiques, small, intimate stores with well-made merchandise and high price tags. Impulsively, she drove over there, parked the van, and strode into the exclusive shopping area.

One shop boasted a gold-scrolled door with the name MOKI-HANA etched on it in black. Krystal pushed open the door and stepped inside, and was almost overwhelmed by the Hawaiian patterns and styles.

A dark-haired woman walked out from a curtained doorway in the back of the store, smiling widely. "You hesitate, miss. But no need. You'd be amazed at the number of mainlanders who like the island styles and fabrics."

Krystal nodded. "It's not what I want, though." She started to turn away. "I shouldn't have come in—"

"Of course you should have." The woman moved to intercept her, taking Krystal's arm in the lightest of grips. "Come into the back, and let me show you some things. You could find something."

The back room was huge. Krystal was dumbfounded. She'd expected to see only bolts of island fabrics. But she also saw spacious dressing rooms, with patrons in them. Beyond that was a bank of sewing machines humming away. Attendants scurried every which way, carrying rich cloths and garments. She glanced around at her guide. "Full-scale operation," she murmured.

"Yes. I'm Moki-hana. When I first came from the islands I intended to stick to fabrics and styles of my homeland. But my curiosity and desire to be a great designer drew me further. I've gathered a strong, loyal clientele. And I don't rob them," she finished fiercely, making Krystal smile.

"It works for me," Krystal said, and explained to the woman about her own business. "And, you see, I wanted—needed a nice dress, and my wardrobe is getting sketchy."

"Name a ballpark figure," Moki-hana said, the slang words sounding strange in her singsong Hawaiian accent.

Krystal did, and earned a grin from the owner. She winced. "Too small."

"Not at all," Moki-hana said. "I'll take care of you myself. Come this way."

Krystal stepped gingerly around the small mountains of fabric and the busy staff, then stopped short when she was led into a spacious dressing room. Mirrors hung on every wall and covered the ceiling.

"I like working in here," Moki-hana said. "It's my favorite room." She smiled at Krystal. "Sit down. I'll only be a minute."

Nodding, Krystal sat on the very edge of the gold soda-bar chair, feeling more uncomfortable by the second.

When Moki-hana whizzed back into the room, she forgot her discomfort. The woman was carrying a pile of clothes nearly as large as herself.

"Not all of this is made up, you understand," Moki-hana said, puffing, straining with her burden. With a whush of relief she lowered it onto a table, then straightened, dabbing at her perspiring upper lip with the back of her index finger. "But some of these will be your size. And you could try them on. If you like what you see, you might want to order something."

"I don't have a large clothing budget," Krystal said.

"Not to worry. You have a business. You'll talk to people. That's my best advertisement."

The next hour was a whirl of clothing and fabric, oohs and ahhs, tugging and pinning.

When she was finally done Krystal leaned against the narrow table, damp with perspiration and both elated and depressed at her choices. She'd spent far too much, dipping into her lease money, but she'd felt reckless and wild. "I hope I don't have sleepless nights about this, Moki."

"You won't, you won't," Moki told her, handing back Krystal's credit card.

Laden with bundles and the address of a shoemaker, she left Moki-hana's store and struggled to the van.

Stopping at the shoe store was a fight with herself, but she gave in. "You don't have anything you can wear with those outfits," she muttered.

A man sweeping the sidewalk in front of a hole-in-the-wall shoe store eyed her. "You want somp'n, lady?"

"No," Krystal said, smiling weakly. "I'm arguing with myself. I do that sometimes. My mother did too."

"Umm. Crazy family." The man shrugged and went back to his sweeping.

"You don't know the half of it," Krystal mumbled,

stepping around him and into the small shoe shop.

An old man was in the back hammering on a shoe. He had a green visor on, and a permanent frown. "Speak up," he said to Krystal. "The world's busy, ya know."

"Shoes." She coughed to clear the croakiness from her voice. "Shoes."

"I got 'em. What size, color, style?" he asked, irascibly, then jerked his head at her. "This way."

All at once Krystal had to fight the laughter bubbling up in her. It had been a crazy morning! Along the way she'd met the most interesting people. And unknowingly they'd bolstered her spirits, which had been sagging badly for days.

She bought two pairs of shoes instead of one, and was elated on the ride home—even if she would have to do the "borrow from Peter to pay Paul" routine for a while.

Cullen's car was behind her building when she returned from her junket. Before she could get the van door open, it was wrenched from her hand. She stared down at a scowling Cullen, and the smile fell off her face.

"Something wrong?" she asked.

"Wrong? Hell, yes, something's wrong. Where have you been? I've been calling all day."

"It's only a little past lunchtime."

"All morning, then. Where the hell were you?"

"What is it?"

"Nothing. I wanted to talk to you." He reached into the van and lifted her to the ground.

Irrational fear gripped her. "Are you sure nothing's wrong?"

He pulled her into his arms. "Nothing. Honest. I just couldn't find you. I couldn't work, not knowing where you were, so I came home." He pressed his mouth to her hair. "I wish you'd leave a more involved message on your machine when you do that."

Relief lifted her arms up and around his neck. "I didn't mean to alarm you. I went shopping."

"What? You never go shopping."

His lopsided smile squeezed her heart. "Well, this time I did." She touched his cheek.

He shook his head. "What the hell do I care, just as long as you're safe."

They swayed together, impervious to the chilly, damp air. He pulled her closer, and she held on tight.

"Come inside," he whispered. "I bought yogurts and some thin-sliced ham. The man said his nephew cured it himself, Westphalian style."

"Pumpernickel and horseradish mustard, I hope," Krystal said. She knew she was flushed. It was almost unbearably exciting being with him, chatting, laughing easily. She'd missed it so much, her being ached with the wanting of it. "I'll get my things," she whispered.

Cullen reached past her and grabbed the parcels. "Show me what you bought while we eat." He turned and leaned down to kiss her, liking the way she flushed.

"I bought a lot," she confessed, starting for the back door. "But it was fun. . . . "

"Are you wearing something new for the fundraiser?"

"Yes."

"I look forward to seeing it."

Her legs turned rubbery as she headed up the stairs to the apartment. She wanted to please him, she wanted to cross the barrier that separated them. She wanted to turn to him and tell him that she loved him, that she wanted to be with him, close to him, loving him. Instead she told him she loved ham.

"You're always hungry," Cullen said, "but you never put on weight." He loved her the way she was, he thought. And following her up the stairs was a delight. Her slim, swaying body made desire rise like a flood within him.

"You're always hungry too," she said, chuckling. She ran ahead and opened the apartment door.

He walked past her sideways, balancing the parcels. "Maybe you could model some of these for me."

Red flagged her cheeks. "There wouldn't be time. You have to get back to work."

"Talk me into taking the afternoon off," he said huskily, lowering the parcels to the small table in the living area and turning to her.

Out of breath, shaken to her shoes, she forced a smile. "Maybe I will."

"Do."

"We'd better eat," she said breathlessly. "Otherwise the dog might get the ham." Why had she said such a stupid thing?

He traced her cheek with one finger. "We don't have a dog."

She sighed, distracted for a moment. "I always wanted one. Silly, isn't it?"

"You lived on a farm in Pennsylvania, didn't you?"

She sighed deeply, and made a sweeping half

turn away from him. "Yes. But after my mother died, I spent years traveling with my father. There wasn't the time or place for an animal in our gypsy life." She smiled winsomely. "I didn't mind."

He heard and saw the opposite behind her smile. It angered him to think of how her father had uprooted her, then amiably neglected her when he should have been providing safety and happiness. He slid his arm around her waist, leaning over her.

"We should eat," she murmured, her eyes closed.

"Right." He watched the play of emotions over her face, noting the vulnerability . . . and the yearning. Inch by inch they were drawing closer again.

The lunched on yogurt, wafer-thin ham on pumpernickel with horseradish mustard, and deli pickles. Ambrosia, and the cider they drank was nectar.

"Why does it taste so good?" she asked Cullen. He looked at her, then laughed. "What's funny?" she asked.

"I was wondering the same thing."

"Simple minds run the same way?"

"Great minds, love, great minds." He wasn't going back to work unless she kicked him out, he decided. "Good cider."

"Good apples in Washington," she said.

"What'll we have for dessert?" He put both elbows on the table and leaned forward, gazing at her suggestively. When she blushed, he grinned. "I can see you're reading my mind."

"Anyone could." Her laugh was shaky, her hands trembled. She wanted him with an undeniable hunger. Without thinking, she put her hand out to him.

He caught it in both of his, not taking his eyes from hers. "You're very beautiful." He kissed her palm.

"You ain't seen nothin' yet," she said, her voice trembling despite her attempt at lightness. "Wait until you see me in my new duds."

"I can't wait."

Silence fell between them, though electric messages were being passed by their eyes. Lightning flashed there, clear and sensual. They stood together, as though someone had given them a silent signal. They leaned forward, and their lips touched.

Cullen's heart thundered. Shocked at the fire, the sudden explosion of feeling coursing through him, he slanted his mouth over hers, eager to taste all of her.

Stunned by the power, Krystal closed her eyes, her body swaying to his, vibrating with need. She'd known what Cullen's loving could do to her. That she could have forgotten that force, its enormity, took her breath away. How had she lived without him these many days? He was the breath of life to her.

He released her mouth and trailed kisses down her neck.

"Cullen!" she cried as sensations crashed over her, hot and wonderful.

"Krystal! Darling, I—"

The phone pealed, slicing through the sensuous wonder.

"Don't answer," Cullen said hoarsely, clutching her to him.

They both listened as the answering machine

clicked in. First they heard Krystal's message, then the caller.

"Cullen! It's Gadsden. You have to be there! Harold on the *Mary Bee* was struck by a shifting load. The damn boat's foundering beyond the straits. I called in the helicopters, but they need—"

Cullen grabbed the phone. "I'm on my way." He grimaced at Krystal, then left the apartment on the run.

Krystal dropped her head into her hands, trying desperately to control her rampaging emotions.

Nine

Over the next two days, Cullen was rarely home. The intimacy fled in the concurrent business of their two lives.

Gadsden and Violet arrived in the late afternoon the day of the fundraiser. Cullen had told Krystal the evening would entail dinner, listening to speeches, dancing, and . . .

Krystal sighed as she began getting ready for their evening out. Since they'd almost come together two days earlier, she'd fought to find time with him. But his crisis hadn't been easily solved. He'd worked day and night, and when he was at the apartment, it was only to sleep. At least they'd be together that evening, but there'd be other people around and—

His key! He was home.

She walked out of the bedroom with her robe on, her toilet complete, except for donning the garment she'd be wearing—one of her new ones, which she was eager for Cullen to see.

"Hi," she said.

He grinned, putting a small animal carrier on the floor. "Hi, yourself. Come welcome our new boarder." He opened the carrier, his smile widening at her perplexity. Reaching in, he brought out a squealing, wriggly puffball. "Meet Maggie O'Dea. Irish wolfhound with a royal lineage longer than anyone's you know, and with a very handsome set of parents, I'm told."

Krystal stared at the long-legged creature as it staggered and bumped its way around the room. "Maggie O'Dea. She's beautiful." Crouching down, she reached out her hand. Maggie instantly nipped at her fingers. "Ouch. Your teeth are sharp, Maggie O." Krystal laughed, clapping her hands. "She's beautiful."

Cullen scooped up the puppy and carted her into the small kitchen. "She's not trained yet, so we'll have to cover the floor with papers."

"Oh. Maybe we could use kitty litter. What do you think?"

Cullen shrugged. "I don't know. But I think we should train her as soon as possible." He jerked his head toward his briefcase. "I brought a dog book home with me. That should help."

"Where did you find her?" Euphoria abruptly overwhelming her, she sank down to her knees, clutching her robe. "Is she really ours?"

He turned at the sound of her wistful voice. She was swiping at her teary eyes, the tension evident in every line of her body as she waited for his reply. "She's yours, Krystal. My gift to you."

He saw her fight her emotion, as though it were a deluge she had to hold back. It shook him to see how much it meant to her to have a scraggly puppy who'd do unsociable things in the apartment. "One of my men got her in a barter with another fisherman. His wife had a fit, so he was going to give her away. I bought her. She has papers. And Lem said he'd seen pictures of her parents, and they were beautiful dogs." He frowned slightly. "I forgot to ask him what size she'd be at maturity. I always had mutts when I was a kid, so I'm not up on purebreds. But I imagine she'll be average size. Not too big, not too small. Anyway, she's yours."

"And she's beautiful. An Irish wolfhound. I think I've heard of them."

"Lem says they're one of the oldest breeds known to man, and they were once used for hunting." Cullen grimaced when Maggie O'Dea squatted on the papers he'd spread on the kitchen floor. "There're going to be some uncomfortable moments with her, I think."

"I'll clean it up," Krystal said hurriedly, afraid Cullen might change his mind and take the puppy back. "I don't mind."

He smiled at her. "You like her, and that's good. So do I. But you're all ready for the evening. I'll handle the cleanup."

She glanced at the clock. "You'd better hurry. We're meeting Gadsden and Violet in about forty minutes."

Cullen galloped through the cleanup, then dashed for the shower.

Krystal was glad to stay in the kitchen with Maggie O'Dea. Cullen had given the puppy an old rolled-up sock, and she was worrying it furiously, growling all the while. Krystal was entranced by the puppy's innocent clumsiness, her insatiable curiosity.

She fetched the dog book out of Cullen's brief-case and flipped through it until she found the section on Irish wolfhounds. "Good Lord," she murmured as she began to read. "Goodness. Heav-ens."

She read to the end, then closed the book and looked down at Maggie O. Biggest dog in the world? Ridiculous. She was only a few pounds. "Surely you won't get that big," she said to the dog. "You're so tiny. They must be wrong." She picked up the wriggling pup and laughed. "It doesn't matter. You're staying." Thinking that she might have misread the statistics on Irish wolfhounds, or that perhaps Cullen had made a mistake about the type of dog, she put it out of her mind and walked into the bedroom to finish getting ready.

Cullen dressed in the bathroom. When he came out he found Krystal in the living room, already dressed. "My Lord," he said, pausing in the act of tying his tie. "You look wonderful."

Her outfit was black, not a color he would have expected her to wear, but she looked stunning in it, classy and sophisticated. The velvet top was heavily encrusted with shimmering beads, and the matching skirt fell just to her knees. Black stock-ings and high-heeled black pumps were the final perfect touch.

"You have style and beauty. And I love you." Only when her mouth dropped open did he realize he'd spoken out loud. She swayed, her gaze fixed on him. "It's been said," he whispered huskily, "and I won't call it back."

"Don't." She reached toward him.

He let the ends of the tie drop and strode to her.

"Rowrrr."

The anguished cry had them both turning and rushing into the small kitchen. The pup had somehow wedged his head in the slightly open oven drawer, and was scratching and yowling in terror and anger.

Cullen freed her and turned to Krystal. "She's all right." He frowned. "But I'm sick of being interrupted." Taking the pup, he put her back in the animal carrier, adding a dish of water and some puppy kibble. Then he rose and faced Krystal. "No more. I'm telling you that I love you. And I want to marry you, not just live with you. When we fight we solve it right then, or at least the same day. I won't be separated from you unless you tell me to go."

"I won't." Her body trembling, she walked into his arms. "Oh, Cullen, I was such a fool. I love you, truly I do, and I let my own insecurities get in the way of that."

"Look at me, love." He stared down into her tear-damp eyes. "Marry me, right away, and we'll live anywhere you please."

"I think we should consider a farm. Maggie O'Dea will need one." When he frowned questioningly, she pulled his mouth to hers and didn't let him speak.

They kissed as though they'd been starved for it, as though it was the sustenance they needed to live.

At last Cullen tore his mouth from hers. "I'll make our regrets," he said hoarsely.

Krystal laughed. "We can't." Her hand stroked his cheek. "But we'll make time later." She stared into his eyes. "I do love you, and I want you in my life. I won't make the mistake of running again. I'm staying with you."

"You've made me a happy man. And you can run anytime you choose—just so long as you take me with you."

"That's a promise."

"Dammit, Krystal, we need to stay here."

"I know," she said somberly. "But we have to go."

They looked around the apartment longingly, as though they were leaving heaven.

"It won't be a long evening," Cullen stated.

They left the apartment hand in hand."

"I like my puppy," she said languorously as they drove through the Seattle night.

"When we're married I'm giving you lots of things. I want that."

"Just come home to me. That's what *I* want."

"Don't worry, I will."

She felt girlish, giddy, light-headed. Her life wasn't falling apart. Cullen and she were knitting a new one, together. Happiness was Cullen.

"You're very beautiful, Krystal. Will you keep your name when we marry?"

She blinked at the suddenness of the question. "Actually, I'd like to take your name, except in business." She smiled when he grinned. "And we can move back to Granger House."

He glanced at her. "Whatever you want." Joy made his hands tremble on the wheel. "I don't know how we got to this point, lady, but I'm not letting us go back."

"Me either." Reaching over, she let one finger trace his ear. "And I'll never let you go." Delicious relief filled her when he turned his head and took her finger into his mouth, sucking it for a moment.

"Feel free to handcuff me to you," he said. "I'll move my office into yours."

She laughed softly. "I'm looking forward to going home tonight, Cullen. I'm eager to show you just how determined I am to keep you." When he groaned, she chuckled.

"Damn, I wish we didn't have to go to this fundraiser."

"So do I." She kissed his ear, then smiled dreamily. "I'm happy. I wish I'd had the good sense to talk to you after that first visit to Banks."

He touched her thigh briefly before putting his hand back on the gearshift. "So do I," he said tautly. "I didn't tell you that I confronted him. From what he said, I gather he's been trying to steal clients from his father for months. And if it hadn't been for his father, I would have pasted him one right there in his office, the officious jerk."

Krystal shrugged. "Oh, I could blame him, I guess. But the real culprit was me. I think I was so unsure of our love that the smallest push sent me running. I don't feel that way anymore. I'll fight to keep you, Cullen Dempsey."

"Good. I feel the same." He scowled as he pulled into the parking garage. "Just remember, this is a short evening."

"Don't worry. I intend to drag you out of here by your hair."

Epilogue

Krystal Dempsey opened her eyes and looked straight at her husband's worried face. "I'm fine."

"Yeah," Cullen said hoarsely. He kissed her cheek, his mouth lingering there. "A boy. We had a boy."

"I know. I was there," Krystal said, laughing, then yawning hugely. "At times it felt like an elephant. But I should've known your son would balk at being born. He likes his comfort, just like you." The past year and more since their wedding had been a lesson in happiness for Krystal. She had traveled with her husband, gone out on his boats, shopped for a farm with him, which they had found and made their permanent residence. And she'd laughed—joyously, uproariously, constantly.

"Don't joke about having the baby," Cullen muttered. "I was scared." He frowned down at her, then kissed her eyebrows, her nose, her lips. "You had a damned long labor."

"Good thing I was in good shape. All that working on the farm paid off."

"It was too much for you. One child sounds about right to me."

"Oh, no, you said we should have a dozen." Krystal felt sore, but supremely good and happy. She'd known how concerned he'd been, how scared even. He'd never left her side, helping her in every phase of the difficult delivery, urging, cajoling, comforting.

He winced. "No way. Let's take care of Cullen Gadsden before we contemplate any others." He scowled. "We should've been staying at Granger House. Then we wouldn't have had that damn long drive to the hospital."

"We didn't stay at Granger House because our 'little' Maggie O'Dea, at around a hundred and fifty pounds, is too big for the city." Krystal touched his cheek, smiling fondly at her husband, who'd brought so much into her life. Not only had he helped her with her business the past several months, so that she'd been relatively at east during her pregnancy, he'd showered her with attention, humor, and caring, so that she'd had more joy than she'd imagined there could be.

Marriage to Cullen had been far more than she'd expected. They'd joined their hearts, minds, and bodies, sharing every experience with each other. Cullen had made it plain that life with her was what he wanted.

She had striven to do the same, and her love for

him had grown each day. "I love you, Cullen," she told him now, as she'd done so often since their wedding day.

He smiled. "Ditto, lady. It's been wonderful. And now we have a son." He snapped his fingers. "Violet and Gadsden are waiting at Granger House for news. I'll have to call. They're very excited."

Krystal nodded, yawning again. "I know. Since they've married, they've become our parents, haven't they? Sometimes I forget they're not." She smiled sleepily. "Our son will be very indulged, I think."

"Why not? He's very lovable, like his mom."

"And dad." She stretched up to lock her hands around his neck.

He leaned over her, kissing her. "Life is beautiful with you, wife. You make me so happy—even if you did scare the hell out of me for the last twenty-four hours." Concern etched his face for a moment. "Don't ever leave me, Krystal. I need you." He kissed her again.

"And I need you, always," she said, kissing him back.

As though they had the same thought, they turned to gaze at the small creature sleeping on his tummy in the hospital crib.

"I never thought life could be so full," Cullen murmured.

"Neither did I. I'll never run from life again. There's too much at my fingertips. I learned that . . . the hard way." She kissed him gently. "Not that it wasn't wonderful coming to Seattle and meeting you. It was."

"Yes." He couldn't stop staring at her. "Motherhood has made you even more beautiful."

"Thank you."

"Kiss me and love me, Krystal Dempsey."

"I do and always will. You've given me life."

THE EDITOR'S CORNER

What an irresistible line-up of romance reading you have coming your way next month. Truly, you're going to be **LOVESWEPT** by these stories that are guaranteed to heat your blood and keep you warm throughout the cold, winter days ahead.

First on the list is **WINTER BRIDE**, LOVESWEPT #522, by the ever-popular Iris Johansen. Ysabel Belfort would trade Jed Corbin anything for his help on a perilous mission—her return to her South American island home, to recover what she'd been forced to leave behind. But he demands her sensual surrender, arousing her with a fierce pleasure, until they're engulfed in a whirlwind of danger and desire. . . . A gripping and passionate love story, from one of the genre's premier authors.

You'll be **BEWITCHED** by Victoria Leigh's newest LOVESWEPT, #523, as Hank Alton is when he meets Sally. According to his son, who tried to steal her apples, she's a horribly ugly witch, but instead Hank discovers a reclusive enchantress whose eyes shimmer with warmth and mystery. A tragedy had sent Sally Michaels in search of privacy, but Hank shatters her loneliness with tender caresses and burning kisses. Victoria gives us a shining example of the power of love in this touching romance guaranteed to bring a smile to your face and tears to your eyes.

Judy Gill creates a **GOLDEN WARRIOR**, LOVESWEPT #524, in Eric Lind, for he's utterly masculine, outrageously sexy, and has a rake's reputation to match! But Sylvia Mathieson knows better than to get lost in his bluer-than-blue eyes. He claims to need the soothing fire of her love, and she aches to feel the heat of his body against hers, but could a pilot who roams the skies ever choose to make his home in her arms? The sensual battles these two engage in will keep you turning the pages of this fabulous story from Judy.

Please give a big welcome to brand-new author Diane Pershing and her first book, **SULTRY WHISPERS**, LOVESWEPT #525. Lucas Barabee makes Hannah Green melt as he woos her with hot lips and steamy embraces. But although she wants the job he offered, she knows only too well the danger of mixing business with pleasure. You'll delight in the sweet talk and irresistible moves Lucas must use to convince Hannah she can trust him with her heart. A wonderful romance by one of our New Faces of '92!

In **ISLAND LOVER**, LOVESWEPT #526, Patt Bucheister sweeps you away to romantic Hawaii, where hard-driving executive Judd Stafford has been forced to take a vacation. Still, nothing can distract him . . . until he meets Erin Callahan. Holding her is like riding a roller coaster of emotions—all ups and downs and stomach-twisting joy. But Erin has fought hard for her independence, and she isn't about to make it easy for Judd to win her over. This love story is a treat, from beginning to end!

Laura Taylor has given her hero quite a dilemma in **PROMISES**, LOVESWEPT #527. Josh Wyatt has traveled to the home he's never known, intending to refuse the inheritance his late grandfather has left him, but executor Megan Montgomery is determined to change his mind. A survivor and a loner all his life, Josh resists her efforts, but he can't ignore the inferno of need she arouses in him, the yearning to experience how it feels to be loved at last. Laura has outdone herself in crafting a story of immense emotional impact.

Look for four spectacular books this month from FAN-FARE. Bestselling author Nora Roberts will once again win your praise with **CARNAL INNOCENCE**, a riveting contemporary novel where Caroline Waverly learns that even in a sleepy town called Innocence, secrets have no place to hide, and in the heat of steamy summer night it takes only a single spark to ignite a deadly crime of passion. Lucy Kidd delivers **A ROSE WITHOUT THORNS**, a compelling historical romance set in eighteenth-century England. Susannah Bry's world is turned upside-down when her father sends her to England to live with wealthy relatives, and she meets the bold and dashing actor Nicholas Carrick. New author Alexandra Thorne will dazzle you with the contemporary novel **DESERT HEAT**. In a world of fiery beauty, lit by a scorching desert sun, three very different women will dare to seize their dreams of glory . . . and irresistible love. And, Suzanne Robinson will captivate you with **LADY GALLANT**, a thrilling historical romance in the bestselling tradition of Amanda Quick and Iris Johansen. A daring spy in Queen Mary's court, Eleanora Becket meets her match in Christian de Rivers, a lusty, sword-wielding rogue, who has his own secrets to keep, his own enemies to rout—and his own brand of vengeance for the wide-eyed beauty whom he loved too well. Four terrific books from FANFARE, where you'll find only the best in women's fiction.

Happy Reading!

With warmest wishes for a new year filled with the best things in life,

Nita Taublib

Nita Taublib
Associate Publisher / LOVESWEPT
Publishing Associate / FANFARE

Don't miss these fabulous
Bantam Fanfare titles
on sale in December.

CARNAL INNOCENCE
by Nora Roberts

A ROSE WITHOUT THORNS
by Lucy Kidd

DESERT HEAT
by Alexandra Thorne

LADY GALLANT
by Suzanne Robinson

Ask for them by name.

CARNAL INNOCENCE

By *Nora Roberts*
author of
GENUINE LIES
and PUBLIC SECRETS

Even the innocent have secrets to hide . . .

Strangers don't stay strangers for long in Innocence, Mississippi, as witty, urbane, and beautiful Caroline Waverly is quick to discover. Fame has taken its toll on the celebrated concert violinist, what with grueling tours and high-pressure performances, climaxing in an all-too-public break-up with the world-class conductor who is also her lover.

All Caroline wants from her stay in Innocence is a chance to be out of the spotlight—to live quietly in her family's secluded old bayou home with its lace-curtained windows and shady front porch. But what she is about to learn is that even in a town called Innocence secrets have no place to hide, and in the heat of a steamy summer night it only takes a single spark to ignite a deadly crime of passion.

For the sleepy bliss of Innocence is shattered forever by the deadly strikes of a killer at large, and Caroline falls under the spell of a town with a darkly deceptive nature . . . and a smooth-talking, irresistible Southern Charmer named Tucker Longstreet whose seductive touch awakens her own carnal desires—and ensnares her in a killer's crazed dreams.

A ROSE WITHOUT THORNS

By Lucy Kidd

Set in Eighteenth-century England, A ROSE
WITHOUT THORNS tells the story of Susannah Bry, a young Virginian whose bankrupt
father has sent her to England to her wealthy
relatives there. In this scene Susannah has her
first encounter with Nicholas Carrick, an actor
who will become her lover. . . .

And as the door closed she was the only one inside.
She had determined it: she would not follow him,
moping after him, just because, by chance, she had
once danced with him. *Carrick.* "Damn!" she whispered, scraping wax from the table with her nails; she
did not know why. She looked around at the green-
walled dining chamber with its smoking sconces; at
the rose-colored closet to one side and the row of
doors leading to empty rooms on the other. For all
their luxury—their gilt furniture, their wall panels
painted with cherubs—the rooms had a dusty, neglected air, all the more marked when they were
empty.

   The others had been outdoors, it seemed, an age.
Curiosity overcame her. She stood and walked to the
door, and half opened it.

   "You don't mean to deny," a mild-voiced man, a

barrister, was saying, "that the institution of marriage has its practical *uses*. . . ."

"Ha!" A big, square-built, red-faced man threw back his head, laughing, and while some of the ladies tittered, the barrister queried, "Would you not agree, Mr. Carrick, with Dr. Johnson's words: that 'Marriage has many pains, but celibacy has no pleasures'?"

At the sound of his name again, *Carrick*, Susannah felt her heart begin to pound. *Why should I care?* she thought. A cold wind grazed her shoulders. *What should I care what he thinks on marriage?* The door beside her creaked, and at the sound Carrick's gaze moved up and found her.

"Why, I'm no enemy of marriage," he said, with a lazy nod at the barrister. Again, almost insolently, he stared up, across the terrace. "Why, a happy marriage must be perfection. A rose without thorns. And"—he began to move through the crowd—"you're just as likely of finding it."

Now he faced Susannah. Quickly, before she was able to speak, he reached up to the bosom of her dress and tugged the rose, on its thin stem, free. Her scarf drifted loose, and he caught it.

She felt the cold air on her skin, yet still could not move as, smiling, he wound the scarf around her wrist and tucked the rose into his buttonhole. Her heartbeats sounded in her ears. As she slid back through the door, she forced a smile to her lips. For a second she watched Carrick and the others; then, as the crowd began to stream in again, she ran for the safety of the empty closet.

She hid in that chamber, with its mirrors and pink walls, trying to pull her dress higher, feeling her face go alternately hot and pale. Outside she had been so tongue-tied and foolish. *Because of him?* She heard the chatter in the other rooms growing louder. She leaned against the window frame, watching her reflection in the mirror opposite. For a moment she felt at peace. Then something moved in the smoky light of the doorway.

She looked over, and her heart began to pound again. Carrick was standing there. She could see only a silhouette: a compact body some inches taller than hers, which he held taught, his arms folded, one foot posed before the other. He seemed to consider her, and slowly walked closer.

If he has come to apologize, Susannah thought, *I will be dignified.* She bit her lip, preparing herself.

But she had no time to remember how. Suddenly Carrick was behind her, his body barely, but decidedly, touching hers. He reached for her hands, then took quick hold of them, sweeping them back behind her. He held them there, his fingers tickling, lightly stroking her palms.

"Where is it you come from?" he said, smiling at their twin reflections in the mirror.

The question surprised her. "Here," she said defensively. "And before that—America."

Her heart beat quickly. Because her dress squeezed her waist in so tightly, all the blood surging through her seemed to rush to what was above and below. Her chest rose and fell quickly with her breathing, and she saw Carrick was looking down at her breasts, at the swell of them. She twisted her hands in his. She knew she ought to escape, for she did not know what she was feeling. The embroidery of his waistcoat grazed the bare skin of her shoulders.

He let go of her hands easily, and smiled. "I did not think they grew such wildflowers in America, as you. I had thought the place inhabited by—drab little Puritans, and savages."

"No. I—" She knew he must expect a witty rebuke.

But she had none. She knew also that she was free to escape now, for he held no part of her. But she did not want to escape. He looked into her eyes—his were black pits, lost to her sight—and, with one hand, then the other, reached below the curling edge of her dress. He lifted her breasts above the cloth, stroking their high curves, and the valley between. The lower half of his body moved against hers. And all the blood that had rushed down there, inside her, was set coursing again as he stroked the tips of her breasts. He did not kiss her. Instead, he tilted his head away, watching her. With a questioning glance, then curiously, deliberately, he stepped back, bending to take the tip of her left breast in his mouth. His tongue worked over it, teasing it, and it felt so good, and yet was such torture, that she had to squirm free. She let out a little cry. He pulled away, then, but returned his hands, teasing her nipples, even pinching them until it seemed to her that there was no feeling in her body but exactly there: there, and in that place between her legs where the flesh was moist and swollen, and finally seemed to have a heartbeat of its own. The blood pulsed and seemed to flow upward, spreading, warming her. She let out a deep breath.

She realized now that her eyes had been closed, and when she opened them she saw Carrick smiling, his teeth glinting in the dark. She let out a low sound of fear, not quite a word, and in answer he kissed her quickly on the forehead. He reached inside his frock coat and pulled out her wrinkled scarf, and as she took it, he plucked the rose, too, from his collar and offered it to her. She shook her head, on a sudden impulse.

He said, "A token?" and smiled back, tucking the rose back into his collar as he left her.

She did not know how long it took for her

breathing to slow, for the color to leave her face. When she had stopped trembling, and righted her scarf and gown, she emerged into the dining chamber, now empty. She knew that her skin was damp, that the paint must be running down her face; but when she saw the others in the next room, she knew they would not notice.

DESERT HEAT

By Alexandra Thorne

A LAND OF FLAMES . . . It is a world of fiery beauty and shadowy dangers, where the arid heat of day ignites the sizzling passions of night . . . and where three very different women pursue their dreams of glory—and irresistible love.

WOMEN OF FIRE . . . Liz, Archer, and Maryann—under an endless sky, lit by sparks, three women ripe with yearning will dare to seize their dreams—but will they be strong enough to keep from getting burned by . . . DESERT HEAT?

In the following excerpt, gallery owner Liz Kant is dining at a restaurant with her lover, Alan, an Apache artist. . . .

She embodied the eternal female mystery—unknowable, unfathomable, and utterly desirable. Tonight she wore a simple black sheath, suspended from her shoulders by narrow straps he had been aching to lower all through dinner.

Liz's coloring made her a painter's dream. She had

flawless ivory skin and shoulder-length, coppery hair framing a face whose perfection still startled him even though ten years had passed since he first saw it. The chiseled planes of her high cheekbones and narrow, slightly aquiline nose offered a fascinating contrast to full, sensual lips that blushed coral without the benefit of makeup. Her eyes were her finest feature. Set beneath well-arched brows and fringed with jet-black lashes, her eyes were the same astonishing shade of blue as Bisbee turquoise.

"I want to make love to you," he blurted out.

"Here?" Mischief sparked in her eyes. "What am I? Dessert?"

"I'll make a fool of myself if we stay here much longer." Reaching for his wallet, he put three fifty-dollar bills on the table. In his haste, he almost knocked his chair over as he got to his feet.

Liz smiled, but her speed matched his as they hurried from the restaurant.

Ten minutes later Alan turned his Blazer onto the steep road that led to Liz's mansion halfway up the flank of Camelback Mountain. He drove automatically, pulled up in front of the house, and walked Liz to the door, while mentally rehearsing what he intended to say later in the evening.

"I want to tell Rosita I'm home, and check for messages," Liz said as he shut the front doors behind them. "How about getting a bottle of champagne and meeting me in the bedroom?"

"Now, that's an offer I can't refuse," he replied. Although he took time to return to his car and retrieve a jeweler's box from the glove compartment, Alan arrived in Liz's bedroom before she did. He set a silver tray bearing a chilled bottle of Perrier-Jouet and two Waterford flutes on the table in front of the fireplace. Then he removed the box from his khaki safari jacket and placed it on the table as well.

Six months before he'd commissioned his friend Ted Charveze, the internationally acclaimed Isleta Pueblo gemologist, to make something special for Liz. Charveze had spent weeks finding exactly the right Bisbee turquoise, flawless stones with depth and *zat.* "Good diamonds are a hell of a lot easier to come by these days than top-notch turquoise," Charveze had complained, "especially when you insist the stones match Liz's eyes."

The results had been worth waiting for. Charveze, who designed for Cartier, had outdone himself, producing a golden, jewel-inlaid collar that took the form of Avanyu, the sacred life-giving serpent. Now Alan opened the box one last time, adjusting the masterwork in its satin-lined lair. Although money meant little to him personally, he enjoyed being able to give Liz beautiful things. Tonight he wanted to envelop her in his love. The excellent meal and the gift were only a part of the pleasure he planned.

Years ago, when he and Liz became lovers, he quickly realized how little she knew of passion. The first time they went to bed she had faked her orgasm— and not very well at that. Back then, he'd still been a bit in awe of her success, the ease with which she moved through the glitzy world of high-priced art. But that night he pitied her. To be a stranger to her own body, a body so perfectly crafted for sensual delight, seemed a tragedy. It still astonished him that Anglos, despite their cultural preoccupation with sex, could be so untutored in the ways of a man and a woman.

Liz had taught him how to get along in the white world, how to dress, to make small talk, to order in the five-star restaurants she liked to frequent—where being seen at the right table with the right people was more important than filling an empty stomach. In return he brought her, slowly and patiently, to the full realization of her womanhood. Now he was as comfortable dealing with a sommelier as if he'd been to the manner born, and she reveled in the pleasures of the bedroom like the most knowledge-able Apache female. It was, he thought, a fair exchange.

Taking off his jacket, he sat in one of the large armchairs that flanked the fireplace. Liz's bedroom was almost as familiar to him as his own, but he never felt quite at ease in it. His own home was built of adobe and furnished in a rough, masculine fashion, with antiques from Santa Fe, Chimayo rugs, and artifacts from the numerous Indian cultures of the Grand Chimeca. By contrast, Liz's room was ostentatiously, sensually feminine. The walls were mirrored, the floor covered with a thick white Aus-tralian wool carpet. The furniture was white too, pickled oak custom-made to Liz's specifications. A quilted, white silk spread covered her oversize four-poster.

The room had been designed as a backdrop for the painting that hung over the fireplace, a four-by-eight-foot portrait of Liz, nude, lying on her bed as if she waited for a lover. As Alan studied the painting, satisfaction warmed his eyes. The portrait, finished six years earlier, had held up well. It was still one of his best works. He'd come very close to doing Liz justice, even though it had been distracting as hell to paint her like that. Grinning, he recalled how much faster he would have completed the canvas if he hadn't stopped so many times to make love to her.

He had wanted Liz from the day he walked into her

gallery. Then, his reaction had been immediate, visceral—desire triumphing over reason. He had never expected to have her, to love and be loved by her. As an impoverished Apache artist, he'd known the Liz Kants of the world were out of his reach.

He'd grown up well schooled in hatred and distrust of whites. His tribal elders had taught that white men had taken everything from the Apaches, their ancestral hunting grounds, their culture, their freedom—even their lives in the bloody, desperate battles of the late 1800s, when government policy had insisted that the only good Indian was a dead Indian. The warrior's death roll—Mangas, Colorado, Victorio, Geronimo, as well as Alan's own ancestors, Cochise and Nachez—was still repeated around countless campfires.

In accordance with his earliest training, Alan had expected to fall in love with a woman of his own people, a girl whose character and fortitude had been tested in the ceremony of the White-Painted Woman, to marry her and have many children as his brothers and sisters had, and to raise them as true Apaches.

Then he'd met Liz, and his expectations had changed irrevocably.

"You look a million miles away," she said, walking into the room and closing the doors behind her. "Is something wrong?"

"I was thinking about us." He paused. This was a momentous evening, and he wanted to do things properly. "I want to talk about our future. But first I have something for you." Taking the case from the table, he placed it in her hands.

Her matchless eyes widened as she opened it. "It's beautiful, Alan," she said throatily, lifting the necklace and clasping it around her neck.

Although he longed to take her in his arms, he poured two glasses of champagne and placed one in her hand. "I've been waiting to talk to you all night. Why don't we sit down."

Liz put her glass down and moved so close to him that her breasts brushed his chest. "I want to thank you properly first."

Enter Loveswept's
Wedding Contest

AH! WEDDINGS! The joyous ritual we cherish in our hearts—the perfect ending to courtship. Brides in exquisite white gowns, flowers cascading from glorious bouquets, handsome men in finely tailored tuxedos, butterflies in stomachs, nervous laughter, music, tears, and smiles. . . . AH! WEDDINGS!! But not all weddings have a predictable storybook ending; sometimes they are much, much more—grooms who faint at the altar, the cherubic ring bearer who drops the band of gold in the lake to see if it will float, traffic jams that strand the bride miles from the church, or the gorgeous hunk of a best man who tempts the bride almost too far. . . . AGHH!! WEDDINGS!!!

LOVESWEPT is celebrating the joy of weddings with a contest for YOU. And true to LOVESWEPT's reputation for innovation, this contest will have THREE WINNERS. Each winner will receive a year of free LOVESWEPTs and the opportunity to discuss the winning story with a LOVESWEPT editor.

Here's the way it goes. We're looking for short wedding stories, real or from your creative imagination, that will fit in one of three categories:

1) THE MOST ROMANTIC WEDDING
2) THE FUNNIEST THING THAT EVER HAPPENED AT A WEDDING
3) THE WEDDING THAT ALMOST WASN'T

This will be LOVESWEPT's first contest in some time for writers and aspiring writers, and we are eagerly anticipating the discovery of some terrific stories. So start thinking about your favorite real-life wedding experiences—or the ones you always wished (or feared?) would happen. Put pen to paper or fingers to keyboard and tell us about those WEDDINGS (AH)!!

For prizes and rules, please see rules, which follow.

BANTAM LOVESWEPT WEDDING CONTEST
OFFICIAL RULES

1. *No purchase necessary.* Enter Bantam's LOVESWEPT WEDDING CONTEST by completing the Official Entry Form below (or handprinting the required information on a plain 3" x 5" card) and writing an original story (5–10 pages in length) about one of the following three subjects: (1) The Most Romantic Wedding, (2) The Funniest Thing That Ever Happened at a Wedding, or (3) The Wedding That Almost Wasn't. Each story must be typed, double spaced, on plain 8 1/2" x 11" paper, and must be headed on the top of the first page with your name, full address, home telephone number, date of birth, and, below that information, the title of the contest subject you selected when you wrote your story. You may enter a story in one, two, or all three contest categories, but a separate Entry Form or Card must accompany each entry, and each entry must be mailed to Bantam in a separate envelope bearing sufficient postage. Completed Entry Forms or Cards, along with your typed story, should be sent to:

    BANTAM BOOKS
    LOVESWEPT WEDDING CONTEST
    Department NT
    666 Fifth Avenue
    New York, New York 10103

    All stories become the property of Bantam Books upon entry, and none will be returned. All stories entered must be original stories that are the sole and exclusive property of the entrant.

2. *First Prizes (3).* Three stories will be selected by the LOVESWEPT editors as winners in the LOVESWEPT WEDDING CONTEST, one story on each subject. The prize to be awarded to the author of the story selected as the First Prize winner of each subject-matter category will be the opportunity to meet with a LOVESWEPT editor to discuss the story idea of the winning entry, as well as publishing opportunities with LOVESWEPT. This meeting will occur at either the Romance Writers of America convention to be held in Chicago in July 1992 or at Bantam's offices in New York City. Any travel and accommodations necessary for the meeting are the responsibility of the contest winners and will not be provided by Bantam, but the winners will be able to select whether they would rather meet in Chicago or New York. If any First Prize winner is unable to travel in order to meet with the editor, that winner will have an opportunity to have the First Prize discussion via an extended telephone conversation with a LOVESWEPT editor. The First Prize winners will also be sent all six LOVESWEPT titles every month for a year (approximate retail value: $200.00).

    Second Prizes (3). One runner-up in each subject-matter category will be sent all six LOVESWEPT titles every month for six months (approximate retail value: $100.00).

3. All completed entries must be postmarked and received by Bantam no later than January 15, 1992. Entrants must be over the age of 21 on the date of entry. Bantam is not responsible for lost or misdirected or incomplete entries. The stories entered in the contest will be judged by Bantam's LOVESWEPT editors, and the winners will be selected on the basis of the originality, creativity, and

writing ability shown in the stories. All of Bantam's decisions are final and binding. Winners will be notified on or about May 1, 1992. Winners have 30 days from date of notice in which to accept their prize award, or an alternative winner will be chosen. If there are insufficient entries or if, in the judges' sole opinion, no entry is suitable or adequately meets any given subject as described above, Bantam reserves the right not to declare a winner for either or both of the prizes in any particular subject-matter category. There will be no prize substitutions allowed and no promise of publication is implied by winning the contest.

4. Each winner will be required to sign an Affidavit of Eligibility and Promotional Release supplied by Bantam. Entering the contest constitutes permission for use of the winner's name, address, biographical data, likeness, and contest story for publicity and promotional purposes, with no additional compensation.

5. The contest is open to residents in the U.S. and Canada, excluding the Province of Quebec, and is void where prohibited by law. All federal and local regulations apply. Employees of Bantam Books, Bantam Doubleday Dell Publishing Group, Inc., their subsidiaries and affiliates, and their immediate family members are ineligible to enter. Taxes, if any, are the responsibility of the winners.

6. For a list of winners, available after June 15, 1992, send a self-addressed stamped envelope to WINNERS LIST, LOVESWEPT WEDDING CONTEST, Department NT, 666 Fifth Avenue, New York, New York 10103.

OFFICIAL ENTRY FORM

BANTAM BOOKS
LOVESWEPT WEDDING CONTEST
Department NT
666 Fifth Avenue
New York, New York 10103

NAME _____

ADDRESS _____

CITY _____ STATE _____ ZIP _____

HOME TELEPHONE NUMBER _____

DATE OF BIRTH _____

CONTEST SUBJECT FOR THIS STORY IS: _____

_____

SIGNATURE CONSENTING TO ENTRY _____

_____